YOU ALWAYS TRY TO KILL ME IN YOUR DREAMS

CARLTON MELLICK III

ERASERHEAD PRESS
PORTLAND, OREGON

ERASERHEAD PRESS
P.O. BOX 10065
PORTLAND, OR 97296

WWW.ERASERHEADPRESS.COM

ISBN: 978-1-62105-332-3

PRAISE FOR
CARLTON MELLICK III

"Easily the craziest, weirdest, strangest, funniest, most obscene writer in America."
—*GOTHIC MAGAZINE*

"Carlton Mellick III has the craziest book titles... and the kinkiest fans!"
—CHRISTOPHER MOORE, author of *The Stupidest Angel*

"If you haven't read Mellick you're not nearly perverse enough for the twenty first century."
—JACK KETCHUM, author of *The Girl Next Door*

"Carlton Mellick III is one of bizarro fiction's most talented practitioners, a virtuoso of the surreal, science fictional tale."
—CORY DOCTOROW, author of *Little Brother*

"Bizarre, twisted, and emotionally raw—Carlton Mellick's fiction is the literary equivalent of putting your brain in a blender."
—BRIAN KEENE, author of *The Rising*

"Carlton Mellick III exemplifies the intelligence and wit that lurks between its lurid covers. In a genre where crude titles are an art in themselves, Mellick is a true artist."
—*THE GUARDIAN*

"Just as Pop had Andy Warhol and Dada Tristan Tzara, the bizarro movement has its very own P. T. Barnum-type practitioner. He's the mutton-chopped author of such books as *Electric Jesus Corpse* and *The Menstruating Mall*, the illustrator, editor, and instructor of all things bizarro, and his name is Carlton Mellick III."
—*DETAILS MAGAZINE*

Also by
Carlton Mellick III

AUTHOR'S NOTE

I had a friend once who seriously believed that if you die in a dream you'll die in real life. I guess he thought that the shock of being killed in a dream would give you a heart attack or something. I'm not sure. But I've never believed it because I die in my dreams all the time. In fact, I die in *most* of my dreams. I've been shot, stabbed, run over, decapitated, strangled, and bludgeoned to death. I've been killed in tidal waves, car accidents, tornados, nuclear explosions, alien invasions and werewolf attacks. I also tend to fall off of cliffs an awful lot, which might be my least favorite way to die in my dreams. Either that or falling into a trash compactor. But after all of these deaths in my dreams I've never once died in real life. At the time of writing this, I'm definitely still alive. So I can assure everyone that this myth is a complete falsehood. Still, the idea of dying in dreams is an often used trope in fiction that I've always wanted to play around with. I was raised on *Nightmare on Elm Street* movies and always wanted to see more exploration into dreamworld horror.

You Always Try to Kill Me in Your Dreams started out as a screenplay and ended up as a novella. It's been twenty years since I've written a screenplay so it was a fun experience, but not one I'll likely try again any time soon. Although I learned plotting through screenwriting classes when I was young, it's not really how I prefer to tell stories these days. I like telling stories one sentence at a time, like building a wall brick by brick. There is something empowering about creating a story in scenes rather than words, but it takes away the passage of discovery that you get when writing a straight narrative. Either way, I learned a lot about my writing by taking a different approach and I'm happy I gave it a shot.

So here it is, my 65th book. I hope you enjoy reading it as much as I enjoyed writing it.

—Carlton Mellick III 02/24/2023 2:43pm

CHAPTER
ONE

Elias is an amazing artist. At least he likes to think he is. His art teacher in high school used to say he was going to be somebody important someday. Maybe not the next Jackson Pollock or Andy Warhol, but somebody who would one day turn the art world on its ear. He isn't sure if she told him this because she really meant it or if she was just trying to be nice and encouraging as teachers are supposed to be. Nobody else in his life has ever said anything as encouraging to him. His mother never cared much for his art and his friends always called it tryhard edgelord bullshit because it was so abstract and surreal and didn't ever look like anything in particular.

Even though Elias thinks he has a lot of potential, he's not sure he has what it takes to become a professional artist. He wants more than anything to find peers who respect the kind of art that he creates, people who will give him confidence and motivate him to become stronger and more productive. He is desperate for some kind of validation.

This is why Elias is going to college. He is certain that

he will finally find other people who are as serious about his art as he is. He's certain that there will be instructors who will teach him how to grow and give him everything he needs to make it in the word of fine art.

His mother can't afford to send him to college. Education is far more expensive than it's ever been before, almost twenty times what it was just a decade ago, but Elias is determined to make it work. He's sure that he'll be successful enough as an artist to pay back his loans and his mom not long after graduation. He just has to work hard and do the best that he can and he's certain that all of his dreams will come true.

Elias has never left his small hometown before, not even on a school trip or family vacation. Raised by his single mother, they never had enough money for travel. His mother worked late hours, pulling double shifts at the diner just to keep up with the rent which has nearly doubled every year since the beginning of the pandemic. But now Elias is on a bus traveling across the country all by himself, terrified and excited to become a self-sufficient adult.

The bus ticket was incredibly expensive. It cost his mother all of her spending money. But the bus itself is a piece of garbage and not at all what he was expecting. It's old and constructed from mismatched repurposed parts. It's dirty and overcrowded. People are crammed into twice the vehicle's capacity, wearing several layers of grubby clothing, surgical masks covering most of their faces. Other people hide their mouths in bandanas, deep coat collars, and homemade masks made from old sweaters and coffee filters held together with medical tape. One person in the back wears a gas mask. Several people refuse to wear any masks at all.

The bus is quiet apart from snores, coughs, and the rumbling of the bus's engine that's long overdue for a tune-up. Elias is squeezed against a window, sporting slightly nicer hair and clothing than the other passengers. Even though most of his clothes come from Goodwill, they are clean. He wears a hand-me-down plaid scarf wrapped around his mouth and a swanky overcoat that might have been considered fashionable in the 1970s. The sleeping old man in the seat next to him leans closer, snoring in his face, possibly-infectious drool dripping onto his shoulder. But Elias tolerates the man's snores, staring out the window, daydreaming.

Elias reaches into his coat pocket and finds a crumpled envelope his mother sneaked in as she hugged him goodbye. He opens it and pulls out a letter.

In large poorly-written letters, it reads:

> YOU ONLY GET ONE SHOT AT
> LIFE. DON'T FUCK IT UP.
>   LOVE, MOM.

Elias pulls out a hundred-dollar bill from the envelope,

shakes his head and shoves it into his pocket. He lets the envelope drop to the ground.

Elias walks down a sidewalk, shivering in the early morning cold, his breath visible. He rolls a large amount of luggage behind him, the wheels loud and squeaky. The bags are all different colors, covered in old patches and stickers, and held together with duct tape. The sidewalk is more tent city than walkway. The tents of the homeless stretch as far as the eyes can see on both sides of the road.

Elias' luggage bumps into something sticking out of a makeshift tent. When he realizes that it's a person's legs he's run into, he steps back, terrified that he's offended them.

"Sorry…" Elias says.

But the person doesn't respond or move, deep in sleep. It's like they are used to being bumped into by those who pass on the sidewalk.

Elias isn't accustomed to seeing homeless camps lining the sides of the road. He had no idea how many people lived without homes in the city. There are more unhoused people than he's ever seen in his life on just one block of the street and there are hundreds of blocks in this neighborhood alone.

He keeps moving.

Up ahead, another homeless man is leaning against a light post, sucking on a dirt-caked vape pen. He gets in Elias' path.

"Hey, got any bills on you?" the homeless man asks. "Anything helps."

Elias reaches into his pocket and pulls out the hundred-dollar bill and hands it to him. The homeless man gets out of his way. He looks down at the bill and sneers.

"That's it?" the man asks in an annoyed tone.

The homeless man spits on the sidewalk as he shoves the bill in his pocket. He takes another hit from the vape pen and shakes his head as he exhales.

"Cheap bastard..."

Elias isn't the type who deals with confrontation very well, so he just picks up his pace and continues on his way. He doesn't look back.

When he arrives at Everett University, he's surprised to see that it looks nothing like the brochures he got in the mail or the pictures that he saw online. It looks more like a prison camp than a school. There are large walls surrounding the place covered in graffiti and topped with razor wire. Overstuffed green garbage bags are piled up on the side of the road. Exhausted security guards armed with MR-15s stand by the gates and patrol the interior like they are just looking for any reason to shoot someone.

As Elias passes through the gates, he walks past one security guard who stares him down while gripping his rifle tighter. Elias realizes he's staring and looks away, avoiding eye contact.

"Keep a distance of ten feet," the security guard says.

Elias isn't sure if he's stating pandemic rules or if students need to stay ten feet away from the armed guards. Because the security guard isn't even wearing a mask, he assumes it's the latter.

As Elias drags his luggage across the campus, he's surprised by how empty the place is. He doesn't see any other students wandering about. Just more security guards on patrol. He wonders if some kind of curfew is in effect.

A female voice comes on the intercom system, broadcasting across campus. The voice announces: "Attention all students. This is a protest-free zone. Participation or organization of political activism on campus may result in expulsion or possible incarceration."

After hearing this, Elias thinks it's odd that protesting isn't allowed on campus. He thought college was all about activism. He's not really the type who gets involved in protests but assumed that it was going to be pretty commonplace once he got to college. He even thought that maybe he would get involved politically if he made any friends who encouraged him to. But now he knows that it's not something that happens at universities anymore. He's beginning to think his college experience is going to be much different than he imagined it would be.

The message repeats: "Attention all students…"

Elias looks down at his phone and up at a tall student dorm several stories high. The place is dark and empty. The windows are boarded up. Graffiti covers the door. It appears long abandoned. A scruffy student steps out of the shadows and sits on a bench near Elias, dark circles under his eyes as though he's been up all night. He sucks on a vape pen and blows it at the ground. Elias turns to him, but doesn't get too close.

"Is this Crestridge Dorm?" Elias asks him.

The scruffy student gives him a dirty look and says, "Kill yourself."

Elias turns away from him and goes to the door, looking around until he notices a card-scanner. He pulls up an app on his cell phone with his Everett University student ID photo. He swipes his phone across the scanner, but nothing happens. He nervously looks back at the scruffy student behind him and then tries again. The doors unlock with a loud click and he hurries inside the dimly lit lobby.

The interior of the dorm is just as rundown as the outside with graffiti all over the walls, half the lights burned out, and beer cans and fast food bags thrown about the place. The carpet is stained with a combination of beer, vomit, coffee, and urine. Elias walks slowly through the fifth-floor hallway, the squeaky wheels of his luggage echo behind him, his eyes darting between his cell phone and the numbers of every door he passes.

He walks by one door that is open, but sees only darkness and clutter. He passes another door that has been ripped off the hinges and now lies on the floor, covered in sticky black fluid and half-eaten french fries. A large naked student steps out of a room up ahead. He wears nothing but a gas mask on his head, rubber gloves on his hands, sandals on his feet, and a towel draped over his shoulder. He struts down the hallway toward Elias. As they pass each other, the naked student kicks Elias' luggage out of his way.

"Racist," the naked student says.

Elias looks back. "Excuse me?"

The naked student punches open the entrance to the bathroom, then scratches his ass as he steps inside. Elias goes back to studying the door numbers and stops at room 534.

"Is this it?" he asks, even though there's no reason to doubt himself.

Elias opens the door to his room and steps onto a concrete floor full of clutter: open suitcases, books, and shoes spread all over the room, clothes draped over the chairs, beds, and desks. Noises come from inside a half-open wardrobe, the sound of somebody digging around in a box of coat hangers. Elias stays in the doorway, but leans inside as far as he can, peeking in the direction of the noise.

He calls out, "Hello?"

A voice responds to him. "Hold on a sec…"

After a couple of minutes, a girl who's at least two years older than Elias backs out of the wardrobe. She wears a bright purple robe and not much else. Her hair wet as though she just got out of the shower. A stack of coat hangers in one hand. When Elias sees her, his eyes light up in surprise. He takes a step back.

"Oh, sorry," he says. "I think I've got the wrong room…"

He looks down at his phone and then at the number on the door.

"It says I'm in room 534."

The girl steps forward. "Are you Elias?"

"Uh… Yeah."

The girl tosses the coat hangers on a bed and goes to Elias and shakes his hand. When she pulls away, he looks at his hand like it might be full of viral germs and wipes it on his coat.

"Hi," the woman says. "I'm your roommate. Nice to meet you."

She picks up a mug of steaming coffee and takes a sip. The mug is multi-colored and oddly shaped as though it was made in an elementary school pottery class.

"Sorry about the mess," she says. "I'm still unpacking."

She kicks her stuff out of the way so that Elias can wheel his luggage inside. He follows the open path she creates, but then stops in the middle of the room. A look of confusion stuck to his face.

"I didn't realize this was a co-ed dorm," he says.

"Oh, it's not. The school thinks I'm a guy so they

19

always put me in the men's dorm."

Elias looks at her with a confused face. "Why do they think you're a guy?"

"Because my name is Robert," she responds. "Whoever registered me into the school system must have assumed I was a guy without even checking. It happens all the time."

The girl returns to unpacking. She takes clothes from her bed and puts them on coat hangers and hangs them in her wardrobe. Elias just stands there awkwardly in the center of her clutter, watching her unpack.

"Your name is Robert?" he asks.

"A typo on my birth certificate. It was supposed to be Roberta, but my mom decided to keep it. She thought it would be cool to have a daughter named Robert. I just go by Roe."

"Roe? Like salmon eggs?"

"Uh… yeah, I guess."

Elias nods.

There is an awkward moment of silence as Roe returns to unpacking and Elias just stands there, not sure what to say.

He breaks the silence to ask, "So are you going to tell them?

"Tell them what?" Roe asks.

"That you're a girl," Elias explains. "I mean, you can't just live in the men's dorm. You have to tell someone."

Roe chuckles, stuffing a handful of underwear in a nightstand. "Yeah, I gave up on that after my first year. All my requests just get ignored. Nobody cares here."

"Seriously?" Elias asks.

"I've gotten used to it. Everyone here just assumes I'm someone's girlfriend."

"So you use the same bathroom as the men? The same shower?"

"Nobody has complained so far," Roe says.

There's another moment of awkward silence as Roe continues unpacking.

When she notices Elias staring at her for an uncomfortable length of time, she says, "I hope you're not going to be weird on me. My last dorm mate was a creep. Always staring at me and touching my hair while I was sleeping. Ew."

She shakes off creepy memories. Then turns to Elias, pointing at him with a wad of bras in her hand. "We're stuck together so let's make the most of it. Just pretend I'm another guy."

Elias looks uneasily at the bras in her hand. "Uh… okay…"

Roe points to the bed on the other side of the room. "This is your bed. Here, let me clear it off for you."

She puts the wad of bras in her teeth and grabs all the clothes that were spread out on his bed. She adds the clothes to the stack on her own mattress and spits out the bras into the nightstand drawer. A trail of drool flows down her chin. She wipes it off and turns back to Elias.

"Make yourself at home."

Elias is completely unpacked. He is just finishing making his bed so neatly that it would pass a military inspection. He closes his drawers full of socks folded Marie Kondo style. He straightens a stack of papers on his desk and places three pens precisely adjacent to the papers. Once everything is absolutely perfect, he turns to Roe lying on her bed messing around on her phone, listening to clearly-audible Kpop on her earbuds. She has barely made a dent in unpacking and her clothes are still scattered about the place. Most of her clothes are getting wrinkled underneath her on the bed. When she notices he's finished unpacking, she pulls the earbuds out of her ears, the music still playing loud enough to hear.

"Hey, want to get some beer?" Roe asks.

Elias is uncomfortable with the question. "Um… Don't we have class tomorrow?"

"Yeah, so? When's your first class?"

Elias picks up his class schedule. "My classes start first thing in the morning."

"Are you serious?" Roe asks.

She gets off her bed and goes to him. She pulls the schedule out of his hand and examines it carefully.

"English at eight ten. Math at nine fifteen. History at ten thirty. Are you a dumbass? You never schedule classes before noon."

Elias shrugs. "I wanted to take all my classes early so I could have the afternoon free to study."

Roe chuckles.

"Study? You don't have to waste your time studying. Classes are stupid easy here."

She examines his schedule more closely. "Hey, we're in the same art class together. How'd you get into figure drawing as a freshman?"

"I took AP art in high school," Elias explains. "They let me skip some classes."

Roe tosses his schedule aside. Elias grabs for it but misses and it floats into a suitcase full of Roe's socks.

"Well, whatever," Roe says. "Nothing happens on the first day of class anyway. Do you have any money?"

"Not really. Only ten thousand dollars."

"That's it? Well, it should be enough for a cheap six-pack. I'll call Jake. He's got a fake ID."

Elias nods. He has no desire to drink the night before his first day of college but it's clear to him that Roe is not the kind of person that's easy to say no to. He just sits on his bed as she texts her friends and makes plans for their evening. He wonders what college is going to be like with Roe as his roommate. It's great that she's also an art student, but how is he supposed to live with a girl as a roommate? He won't be able to change his clothes in front of her and can't just sleep in his boxer shorts. What if he farts in his sleep or she catches him masturbating? It all seems too uncomfortable for him to bear. She seems nice and is far more attractive than the girls back home, but he has no idea how he's going to deal with sharing a room with her for a full year.

Elias doesn't want to hang out with Roe's friends on his first night on campus, but he couldn't wiggle his way out of it. He's now sitting on a dorm room floor with three guys he doesn't particularly feel comfortable around. They look and act like the jocks he knew back home, but for some reason, they are dressed in next-level hipster attire. There's Jake, wearing an unbuttoned Hawaiian shirt, a red scarf wrapped around his neck, orange sunglasses on his forehead, sitting cross-legged. A shorter guy named Mikel is in a full lime green suit with a neon pink baseball cap on his head. Then there's Gregory, spread out across the floor with camouflage pants, a tie-dye bandana he wears like a bib, and a moth-eaten Cosby sweater.

The room is in even worse condition than the one Elias has been assigned to. The unsheeted mattresses are covered in several years' worth of stains. The ceiling drips brown water into a bucket in the corner. The desks are carved up with ages-old messages and covered with marker scribblings. It's like the dorm hasn't had any maintenance or janitorial staff in over a decade.

Elias sits awkwardly off to the side, not saying a whole lot to anyone. Roe, on the other hand, is in the direct center of the group, laughing her ass off and chugging a beer. They are playing a drinking card game called Asshole that Elias has never heard of before. Jake is in the position of president. Roe is vice president. Elias is the asshole. He doesn't understand the game at all yet.

Jake points at Elias. "Drink, asshole."

Elias looks down at his can of cheap beer that he's barely touched. Then he looks at Jake, confused.

"Why do I have to drink? I didn't break a rule."

Roe gives him a sympathetic look. "You're the asshole, Elias. You have to drink whenever the president tells you to drink."

"This game is confusing," Elias says.

He takes a painful swig of the foul-tasting fluid.

Everyone else chants: "Drink. Drink. Drink."

Jake shuffles the deck of cards and begins dealing out a new hand.

He says, "So, as your president, my new law is that you have to drink every time you're caught checking out Roe's tits."

Roe kicks Jake in the knee so hard that he spills his beer.

"Fucking racist creep. What kind of rule is that?"

Jake laughs and cleans his spilled beer with a random shirt.

Mikel says, "He's president. He can make any rule he wants."

Roe adds, "Well, as vice president I'm making the rule that in addition to drinking I get to kick your ass if I catch you checking out my tits."

She shoves Mikel with the heel of her foot. "Especially you, Mikel, you fucking perv. Don't think I forgot about how you barged in on me while I was taking a shower last year."

Mikel laughs. "It was an accident. I swear."

"Bullshit," Roe says, organizing the cards in her hand.

Elias looks at Roe and lets out a sigh, empathizing with her for having to deal with these douchebag guys for the past couple of years. Jake catches Elias looking at her and points his finger furiously, his butt hopping up and down off the floor.

Jake cries, "Hey! The asshole is checking out Roe's boobs! He has to drink!"

Elias' eyes widen in shock as all the guys in the room look over at him and laugh.

"Busted, asshole!" Mikel yells.

"Drink!" Jake says.

Mikel smacks Elias' shoulder. "Roe gets to kick your ass, too!"

Elias' eyes lock on Roe's. He holds up his hands in protest.

"I didn't, I swear," he says.

Mikel shakes his head. "Don't lie, asshole. We saw you."

"I'm not lying," Elias says.

Mikel and Jake look at Gregory who sits next to Elias.

Jake asks, "What do you think, Gregory? Did he do it or not?"

Gregory is stoned out of his mind and not at all engaged in the conversation. A bored and annoyed look is on his face. When questioned, he shrugs and speaks in a slow calm tone.

"No," Gregory says. "He was just sitting there. Leave him alone."

"Oh, kill yourself," Jake tells him. "He did too."

Gregory shrugs it off. "Whatever."

Roe pretends nothing happened and moves on.

"Okay, children…" She stands up and stretches her legs. "I'm going to the bathroom. You can go ahead and jerk each other off while I'm gone."

The guys boo her and throw crumpled fast food wrappers and dirty socks in her direction as she walks for the exit. Once she leaves, Mikel pulls a few throwing knives out of a sheath strapped to his waist and throws them at a target in the wall behind where Roe was sitting. Elias isn't sure if he throws the knives to look cool in front of the other guys or because he's such a sexually frustrated prick that he always needs to stab something to release the tension. The knives were hidden under his shirt, making Elias wonder if he carries those things around campus with him wherever he goes. Either way, Elias doesn't feel safe around such a person.

With Roe no longer in the room, the guys turn their attention to Elias. They stare at him for an uneasy length of time, like a pack of hungry animals, as he sips his crappy beer in silence.

Jake finishes his beer and tosses it aside in a pile of cans near the sink, then he inches closer to Elias.

"So you're Roe's new roommate?" he asks.

Elias looks up at him sheepishly.

"Uh… Yeah, I guess," Elias responds. "I didn't think I was going to have a girl as my roommate… It's kind of weird."

Jake frowns at him. "Weird? Kill yourself, dude. You hit the jackpot."

Mikel adds, "Yeah, you're the luckiest guy in the

dorm. I'd kill to have Roe as my roommate."

Elias shrugs. "I don't know. It seems like it's going to be awkward. Where am I supposed to change my clothes?"

"Just change in front of her," Mikel says, throwing his last knife into the target board. "Who cares?"

"What if I snore in my sleep?" Elias asks. "Do I have to go to the bathroom every time I have to fart? What if she catches me masturbating?"

The other guys burst into laughter.

"Can't help you there, bro," Jake says.

Mikel leans closer, lowering his voice in case anyone is listening from the hallway. "You don't get it. Roe is a total slut. She fucks all of her roommates. You're going to have the best year of your life."

Elias' expression is more of concern than excitement. Gregory shakes his head and looks at Elias.

"Those are just rumors," Gregory says.

Mikel punches him in the shoulder. "They're not rumors. Whenever she's drunk and horny she's got a dick right there waiting for her. She'll probably even fuck you tonight."

Jake gets annoyed at Mikel's words. He chugs another beer and throws the empty can against the wall. "Don't listen to him. Mikel's full of shit. Stay the fuck away from her if you know what's good for you."

Mikel laughs his ass off. "You're just saying that because she doesn't want anything to do with you." He looks at Elias. "Jake's been trying to fuck her for two years now and failing hardcore."

Jake narrows his eyes at Mikel.

"Shut up, dude," Jake tells his roommate. "Just shut the fuck up." Then he stares down Elias. "Roe is off limits."

When Roe barges into the room, the men all go quiet and sit up straight. The girl returns to her seat on the floor and picks up her cards. She opens a new beer and takes a chug.

"Come on, losers," Roe says. "Let's get fucked up!"

Jake and Roe clink their beer cans together in a cheers.

"Let's do it!" Jake yells.

But as the alpha male smiles and raises his can in the air, he stares down the new kid with more aggression than Elias has ever felt from another human being in his life.

Elias walks Roe back to their room. She is so drunk that she can't walk on her own and is barely able to stay conscious. He holds her upright, carrying the bulk of her weight. She seems like she'll topple to the floor at any minute without his help.

"Come on," Elias tells her. "We're almost there."

A group of drunken guys break out of a room behind them and scream "Woooo!" in their direction.

Roe turns back, looking over Elias' shoulder, and responds with a "Woooo!" as though she wants to go over to them and continue drinking. But Elias keeps pushing her forward.

The guys look in her direction, waving her over to their dorm room. But once Roe turns away from them, they call her a bitch and go back inside. Roe presses her head against Elias' arm and then looks up at him.

"You're so nice, Eliot," she says.

"It's Elias," he tells her.

She sloppily caresses his cheek, wiping her hand across his eye and forehead, then down his nose and mouth. He pulls his head away. She giggles at his shyness.

"You're a good one," she says, her eyelids drooping. "I think I like you."

When they get to their room, Elias drops her down on her bed. She curls up in the clothes that are still spread across her mattress and pulls them over her like a blanket.

Elias is getting ready for bed. He stands in front of the mirror, brushing his teeth. He glances at Roe, who is lying on her back with her shirt pulled up, exposing her stomach tattoo, belly button piercing, and part of her bra. He quickly looks away, realizing how inappropriate it is for him to stare at her.

"Can you turn the light off?" Roe asks.

He looks back and sees that her eyes are still closed, like she spoke in her half-sleep. Elias pulls the toothbrush out of his mouth and spits toothpaste in the sink.

"Sure." He flicks off the light switch, leaving only a dim lamp on near the desk. Then he goes back to brushing his teeth.

As Roe lets out a deep, satisfied exhale and drifts off

into slumber, a strange sensation ripples through Elias' body. He looks at the hand holding his toothbrush and notices that his limbs are transforming. They are turning to a hazy smoke-like texture. Elias' eyes widen in terror as he struggles to understand what is happening to him.

Just as he's about to cry out, his body loses its shape and becomes a white mist. The toothbrush falls through his ghost-like hand and plops against the floor. And before he can comprehend what is happening or do anything about it, Roe inhales and his entire being is pulled inside of her.

CHAPTER
TWO

Elias materializes on a campus sidewalk. He looks around, wondering how he got here. His hand is still positioned as if holding a toothbrush, but it's empty, and he's outside. He wonders if he drank too much and blacked out. He wonders if he's sleepwalking.

He turns around to see Crestridge Dormitory behind him, but it isn't the same as it was when he arrived that day. The building is crawling with living red vines that slither up its walls and chirp like crickets. There are no lights on inside the dorm. The streetlamps are burned out. It looks like nobody has been on campus for five decades. The sky is especially abnormal. It looks like a massive egg shell cracking and oozing rotten egg yolk toward the ground. The campus seems empty of other people at first, but then Elias notices hulking black figures in the distance. They are unmoving humanoid shadow creatures, facing him, as though waiting to attack if he comes any closer.

Elias hurries toward the dorm entrance and finds two people opening the door to go inside. He recognizes

Roe is one of them.

"Roe!" he calls out.

Roe stops in the doorway and turns back to Elias. He rushes toward her.

"What's going on?" he asks. "How did I get here?"

Roe is just as drunk as she was before, leaning on the person next to her to stand up straight. Her eyes light up with drunken excitement when she sees him.

"Eliot!" she cries. "It's you. What are you doing here?"

Elias looks around at his unusual surroundings. "I have no idea. We were up in our room a minute ago." He looks at the building and the strange sky. "What is going on with this place?"

Roe looks at the person next to her, patting her on the shoulder.

"Hey, hey," Roe says to the woman. "This is my roommate, Eliot."

Elias looks at the person she's leaning on. It is a woman, but she's not quite human. Her face is in shadows, but her form is definitely not right. Something is off about her. Gurgling and wheezing noises come from her direction.

Roe turns to Elias. "Eliot, this is my friend, Ashemedy. She's totally available. You should date her."

The woman steps out of the shadows and Elias can see her more clearly. She's like a mutant. The left side of her face is swollen and pulsating. Tendrils of flesh grow where her hair used to be. Her mouth and nose and eyes are warped and distorted. She looks like she's made of plastic that was melted in the sun.

Elias shakes his head in disbelief when he sees her

and backs away a little. But she steps forward, holding out her hand to shake Elias's.

The woman says, "Efrremmshiy Toookritch Nieff onoswayth."

Elias wrinkles his eyebrows in confusion. "Excuse me?"

"Worshimat nocksford bean titch," the woman says.

Elias looks at Roe. "What's she trying to say?"

Roe doesn't seem to process what is going on, still in a drunken stupor. She leans in close to Ashemedy.

"Isn't he so cute and awkward?" she asks the strange woman. "You should totally hook up with him."

Ashemedy mumbles something to her and they giggle.

Elias is losing patience. "Roe… what is going on? I'm seriously freaking out right now."

Roe continues giggling into Ashemedy's shoulder.

"Let's go upstairs. I want you two to get more acquainted."

As Roe staggers into the darkness of the dormitory, Elias looks back at the broken eggshell sky. The dark figures in the distance seem to be coming closer but he has yet to notice any of them moving. When he turns back to the door, both Roe and Ashemedy have disappeared. He leans into the doorway, looking into the pitch-black lobby.

"Roe? Are you still there?"

No one responds. The place is deserted. Elias walks inside and closes the door. From inside, Elias looks out of the dorm entrance windows, watching as the shadowy figures in the distance close in, surrounding the place like a horde of zombies. He steps away and heads for the front desk of the dorm, but nobody is sitting back there.

"Hello?"

He goes to the elevators. The doors to one elevator are stuck half-open but there's nothing inside. They seem broken. The lights are flickering. Elias goes inside and pushes buttons, but nothing works. Once a black tar substance leaks down the elevator buttons, covering his fingers, he backs away and wipes his hand against his pants. He turns around to see the same black tar leaking down the walls of the elevator. He rushes out and goes toward the stairwell.

When Elias gets to the fifth floor, it's in even worse shape than it had been before. The ground is cracked and warped, coated in a layer of soil that grows black fungus in the corners. The dorm rooms are boarded up. The walls are covered in moss and red vines. Flickering ceiling lights are the only sign that the building isn't completely abandoned.

At the end of the hallway, two figures are wrestling on the ground. Elias steps toward them and calls out, "Hello?"

As Elias moves through the hallway, the same black tar substance from the elevators leaks down the walls. He quickens his pace. When the figures come clearer into view, he sees that it is Roe wrestling Ashemedy to the ground. A long piece of black metal is in Roe's hands. She tries to stab it into Ashemedy's chest as the woman wriggles beneath her.

"Roe?" Elias asks. "What are you…"

Before he gets to them, Roe plunges the blade into

Ashemedy's chest. Ashemedy moans as the blade enters her, as though it is more of a pleasurable experience than painful. Elias stops in his tracks as Roe stabs her three more times, black gore spraying across the walls. Ashemedy cries out in orgasm as she is stabbed to death. When her body falls limp, Roe licks blood from the blade and looks up at Elias.

"Oh, hi, Eliot," Roe asks in a blissful tone.

She looks down at the dead body between her legs and then back up at Elias.

"I'm sorry I killed your girlfriend." Roe puts on a cute innocent face and hides the blade behind her back. "She wasn't good for you anyway. She was infested with worms that would have made you sick and fat with babies."

Elias steps closer and gets a better view of the wounds on Ashemedy's body. Instead of just blood, she leaks tiny worm-like parasites that squirm out of her flesh.

"Come here," Roe says. "I have something for you."

As Elias steps back, Roe jumps to her feet and runs at him with the blade.

"Let's have some fun together," Roe yells.

As she comes at him with the blade, Elias turns and runs.

"What are you doing?" he cries.

Roe laughs as she chases him down the hallway.

She says, "Come on, don't run. Let me cut you a little. I want to see what it feels like."

Elias jumps into the stairwell and falls into a muddy puddle on the floor. The door closes behind him. He stays there on the ground for a moment, catching his breath. Roe doesn't chase after him. He gets to his feet and opens the door. The hallway is empty. He lets out a long exhale and leans against the doorway.

"What the fuck…" he says to the empty hall.

Then he looks around, wondering where he should go and what he should do. His hands won't stop trembling as he rubs black liquid from his face.

Elias is suddenly back in his dorm room, staring at himself in the mirror. The morning sun is shining through the window. Behind him, Roe is getting out of bed.

"You're still up?" she asks. "Didn't you get any sleep?"

Elias looks around the room, wondering where he is. His hands are still shaking.

He says, "Umm… I don't know. I think I fell asleep standing up."

Roe chuckles. "You're so weird." She goes for the door. "Excuse me. I have to pee."

Elias jumps out of her way when she comes toward him, as though scared she's going to stab him to death even though there's no longer a weapon in her hand. She just staggers past him, opens the door, and leaves the room.

He's able to take a deep breath when he has the room to himself. He has no idea what had happened to him or if it was even real. It didn't feel anything like a dream but he can't imagine what else it could've been.

He looks down and picks his toothbrush off the ground. A perplexed look on his face as he stares at the toothbrush, toothpaste dried against the bristles. He washes it off in the sink and puts it away.

When he gets a good look at himself in the mirror, he notices a smear of black fluid on his face. The back of his shirt is caked with mud. He has no idea where it came from.

Elias gets ready for class and leaves the dorm before Roe comes back from the bathroom. She's been in there for quite a while. He wonders if she fell asleep in the toilet stall, but doesn't bother investigating before going for the stairwell and rushing to class.

The classroom is dark with no windows and one door. Old, beaten-down desks and chairs are spread out in uneven rows. Elias takes a seat off to the side toward the front of the room. The students around him are chatting and smiling and fucking around. Many wear face masks and gloves, but several don't even bother since there's no one around to complain. Although everyone in the room is lively with energy, Elias is dazed and exhausted like he didn't sleep at all the night before. He rubs his red eyes and shakes his head awake.

In the front of the class, there is a large projection screen. It lights up and the figure of a large disheveled man wearing a black cloth mask on his face appears, sitting behind a desk, fucking around on his phone. It is a prerecorded lesson. All the kids in the room quiet down and fold their hands on their desks, staring intently at the teacher on the screen. The English teacher looks up at the camera, realizing he's being recorded. He puts his phone away, pulls down his mask, and clears his throat.

"Uh… Welcome to English 101," the teacher says. "I'm your instructor, Mr. Chaver. I'm sure you're all hungover as hell and don't give a shit about what I have to say, but do whatever you need to do and you'll pass the class, I guess. Anyway, your syllabus should be printing now. Do what's on it and you'll be fine. There's some books on there that you have to read and some writing assignments and I guess somebody will look them over or something like that. It's an easy class, so just show up and do what you need to do and you'll pass. Have a great semester."

The teacher raises his mask and goes back to fucking around on his phone. A printer in the front of the room turns on and starts shooting out pieces of paper. The students get up from their seats and line up to take their syllabuses, going back to chatting and fucking around. Elias just sits there, trying to stay conscious. His eyes roll shut and he almost falls asleep until some guy butt-bumps against the back of his head. It freaks him out so much that he nearly falls out of his seat. He swats at the back of his head like a spider is crawling on him and then jumps to his feet. Everyone looks at him and he regains composure. Then he staggers toward the back of the line.

After everyone gets their syllabus, they just leave the room and go back to their dorms. Elias is confused by this. He has no idea why anyone even bothered coming to class at all. The teacher could have just emailed out the syllabus to the students and saved everyone some time.

Because he has another class right after this one, Elias decides to hang out in the room for a while to look over his syllabus rather than going back to his dorm or sitting on a bench somewhere. Even though the class is over, the prerecording of the instructor continues for the full hour. Elias watches him sitting there, messing around on his phone as if he doesn't even realize he's being filmed. He scratches his crotch a couple of times and even farts once. Based on his lewd facial expressions, it seems like he might be watching videos on pornhub or maybe chatting with a cam girl. Either way, Elias is certain that the instructor is unaware he's being recorded until the end of class when the teacher clears his throat and sits up straight.

"So that's all the time we have for today," Mr. Chaver tells the empty classroom. "I'll see you on Wednesday."

And then the screen goes black.

Elias just stares in amazement for a moment and then can't help but laugh. But he doesn't find it funny. He finds it pathetic and insulting. He hopes it won't be like this every day.

Elias takes a long swig of coffee from a paper cup, feeling much more alert and awake than in his earlier classes thanks to a heavy dose of caffeine. He stands behind an easel holding a blank canvas. The classroom is packed with other students behind similar easels, but all the others are already painting and hard at work. The lesson playing on the screen in front of the class is in the middle of its recording. A naked woman is standing there, holding a pose that the students are expected to replicate. Behind the naked woman, a teacher is instructing the class. It is the same teacher from Elias' English class, only now he calls himself Mr. Carver.

"So, yeah, draw the model using charcoal pencil or ebony pencil or whatever you got," he says.

The teacher points out the curves of the woman's hips and breasts.

"Make sure to get the right angle and do a good job when you draw her boobs and everything. If you're not comfortable drawing a naked woman feel free to do clown faces or beach balls or whatever instead of boobs. I don't care. Just draw something."

All the other students in the room are well into their drawings, working quickly and confidently, and completely comfortable in this environment. Elias, on the other hand, is hesitant and awkward, his hands still trembling. His canvas is still blank. He draws one line that represents the curve of the woman's body with a graphite pencil, but then pauses, shakes his head, and tries to erase it with a big gray eraser. It only smudges across the canvas. As Elias leans back and sighs, Roe comes up behind him and grabs him by the shoulders. He jumps in shock.

"I'm super late," Roe says, not even trying to keep her voice down. "What did I miss?"

She takes the empty easel next to Elias, then removes her backpack and drops it by her feet. Elias becomes visibly nervous in her presence.

"We have to draw the model," Elias says.

He points at the screen.

Roe nods. "Oh yeah. No problem."

The art teacher points at the model's left breast and says, "She's got big boobs so make sure you draw them accurately and to size."

The art teacher gets too close to the model, almost touching her nipple when he points at her. She breaks her pose for a moment and looks at him like she's about to punch him right in the face.

"Get the fuck away from me, racist," the model says.

The art teacher holds up his hands and backs away. The model continues her intimidating posture until he's at a safe distance. Then she returns to her pose.

"Fucking screep," she says.

The art teacher lets out a nervous laugh and turns back to the camera. "Well, just make sure you draw her respectfully. This is art, not pornography."

Then he looks back at the model as though expecting some kind of kudos for his words. When he realizes he's being ignored, the teacher just shrugs and turns away.

Roe goes right into drawing. She looks over at Elias' canvas and back to hers.

"So how has your first day been going for you?" she asks him.

Elias says, "Okay, I guess. But are all classes like this?" He points at the screen. "I thought we'd get a real instructor. Not… this guy. He's not even an artist, is he?"

Roe laughs.

"Yeah, all classes at this school are bullshit," she says. "You don't have to try that hard."

Elias shakes his head in frustration. "It's five million a semester. They don't even have real instructors? Live models?"

Roe shrugs. "Welcome to Everett University."

"I came here for an education," Elias says. "This is bullshit."

"Twenty years of student loan debt for a fourth-rate education? How is *that* bullshit?" She snickers and continues drawing.

Elias looks over at Roe's picture and she's already almost finished. She's shading the figure at a fast pace and the end product is superior to all the other drawings in the room despite her spending only a few minutes on it. Elias inspects her art closely and then looks back at his barely-started work that has more eraser marks than actual lines. He's never felt so pathetic in an art class before.

"How'd you draw that so quickly?" he asks her.

Roe shrugs. "I always draw this fast."

"It's really good," he says.

Roe steps back and tilts her head, examining her picture.

"You think so?" she asks. "I can't really tell. Whenever I draw, my goal isn't to draw anything worthwhile. I just want to finish as soon as possible."

"But wouldn't it be better if you slowed down and took your time?" he asks.

"Hell no. If I go any slower I'll second guess myself and never finish." Roe uses her finger to smear in some extra shadows. "Perfectionism is the death of creativity. It's better to just go for it than worry about whether it will suck or not."

Elias looks at his mostly blank canvas and frowns.

"Besides, they don't grade on quality here," Roe says. "If you draw something you pass. If you draw nothing you fail. Easy choice."

Roe finishes her drawing and steps back, examining her work. She nods her head in acceptance.

"Good enough," she says.

Elias looks over at it. His eyes light up in shock. He's never seen anybody draw something so professional in so little time. He's never even met an art student who could match her level of skill if they had a whole month to complete an image. To say that he's impressed would be an understatement.

"Good enough?" Elias says. "It's amazing. I can't believe you did it so effortlessly."

Roe shrugs. "Meh. Best I could do with a hangover."

She lies down on the floor and rests her head on her backpack.

"What are you doing?" Elias asks.

"Taking a nap." She pulls her jacket over her like a blanket. "Wake me up when class is over."

As Roe closes her eyes and curls up into a fetal position, Elias takes a closer look at her drawing. He glances at the model, then down at her drawing, then to his own sketchpad. He takes a breath and then rushes into a drawing, throwing lines as fast as he can, trying to draw as quickly as Roe did. But after a few minutes, he cringes at the horrible work of art he's creating. He rips out the paper, crumples it up, and throws it away. He lets out a long sigh and starts again on a fresh piece of paper.

Just as he puts his pencil to the pad, Roe falls unconscious and takes a deep breath. Elias' body dematerializes, turning into a smoke-like texture. He looks down at himself with a look of horror on his face.

"Hey… wait!" he cries.

Roe inhales and sucks his smoke-like body inside of her. The other students in the class look back in Elias' direction, startled by his scream, but all they see is his empty easel where he was standing. They shrug and go back to their drawings.

CHAPTER
THREE

Elias finds himself in the same art class he was in a second ago, only the room is brightly lit and mostly empty. The floor, ceiling, and walls are made out of textured canvas paper. All the details of the room, the coat rack full of coats, the books on the shelves, the cubbies of art supplies—they are now painted against the walls like sloppy graffiti. The students in the room have all been replaced by naked mannequins facing blank sketchpads. He seems to be alone.

"What are you doing in here?"

Elias turns to see Roe standing in the doorway. She's holding her sketch pad, coat, and backpack with an impatient look on her face. He becomes startled and confused.

"I have no idea," he responds.

Elias walks over to her.

His voice is in a panic as he says, "I was drawing and then everything in the room turned into canvas paper. All the students are mannequins."

"That's because you're in the wrong room," Roe explains. "Our class is down the hall."

Elias is confused.

She points to her left. "Come on."

Elias goes to her and leaves the room.

The hallway is warped and crooked as they walk through the building. It's no longer a university hallway, more like the hallway of an elementary school. Six-year-old children run about the place. Kid's drawings are posted all over the walls. Big bubble letters spell out sayings that are not exactly English. Some of the letters aren't even from any recognizable alphabet.

"Who are all these kids?" he asks, as children race between Roe and Elias, laughing more like old talking dolls than human beings.

He asks, "Where are we? This isn't even our school."

Roe looks back at him. "Our class is just up ahead."

Elias peeks into the classrooms full of children sitting at small child-sized desks, laughing and cheering at dancing teachers in stuffed animal costumes.

"This definitely isn't our school," he says.

They pass another classroom where a teacher wearing a blue bunny outfit is lying spread out across his desk with his belly slit open and intestines spilling out to the floor. The children sit in their seats with their hands folded, watching the dead man in the bunny outfit as a single small boy licks blood from his blue fur. Elias only glimpses this for a second as he passes the doorway, but doesn't dare go back to verify if what he saw was real.

Roe leads them to a door at the end of the passageway and opens it for them. "Here it is."

Elias goes in first. Once he's inside, he realizes that

it isn't a classroom at all. It is a storage closet. There's only enough room for Elias and Roe to squeeze in and close the door behind them. Three other students are in the room, squished against the back wall. They are faceless and gray.

"This isn't a classroom," Elias says. "It's a closet."

Roe puts her fingers to her lips. "Shhhh… It's about to start."

A screen on the wall right in front of them lights up and a shadowy figure appears. It's difficult to make out. The figure is made out of static. The students stare at the figure for an awkward amount of time. The figure stares back at them.

"What the hell is this?" Elias asks. "What are we doing in here?"

"It's about to begin," Roe says. "Get ready."

Roe is focused. Her eyes narrow. She bends her knees a little as though getting ready to jump.

"Get ready for what?"

As Elias says this, the figure's arm shoots out of the television screen and is driven into the chest of one of the faceless students. Black blood explodes from the person's chest and he falls to the ground. When the figure pulls its arm out of the student's corpse, Elias notices that the appendage is more like a knight's lance than an arm. It is sharp and pointy and hard as steel.

"What the hell!" Elias cries.

"Dodge!" Roe yells.

The figure stabs at the students with its sword-like arm as quickly as it can. The students duck and jump and dodge left and right as they are being attacked.

As he struggles to avoid the assault, Elias asks, "What the hell is going on? Why is the teacher trying to kill us?"

"This is Warrior Class," Roe says. "Of course he's trying to kill us."

"What the hell is Warrior Class?" Elias asks.

"We're training to be warriors!" Roe explains.

The teacher's attacks pick up speed. One faceless student is stabbed through the head as he tries to duck and falls lifelessly to the ground. The other is stabbed in the back as she tries pressing herself against the back wall. Elias and Roe continue to dodge, but Elias finds it difficult to move with the three bodies taking up so much room on the floor.

"Keep going!" Roe cries. "We're almost done!"

Elias trips over a body and falls to the ground. He panics as the figure made of static stabs at him. He lifts the upper half of a dead body to use as a shield while the lance shoots straight for him. He closes his eyes and tenses his muscles, preparing for impact.

"What the fuck!" he cries as the lance-arm is driven through the corpse's chest and into his upper arm.

Elias wakes up back in his art class, standing at his easel. The class is over. Students are leaving the room. They turn their drawings in at a large bin in the front of the class.

"You didn't draw anything?" Roe asks.

Elias looks back at Roe as she sits up and gets to her feet. She yawns and rubs her eyes, just waking up from her nap. Elias looks at his canvas. It is still blank. He looks down at his shirt and notices that he's covered in sweat. His armpits and the front of his shirt are soaked with black blood. His hair is messy and frazzled. He looks like he just stepped off of a battlefield. He is still breathing heavily, exhausted from fighting for his life in the other world.

"Just do something real quick," Roe tells him. "You'll get an F for the day if you don't turn something in."

Elias just stands there, staring at her, trying to catch his breath.

Roe decides to help him out.

"Here, just do this," she says.

She goes to his sketchpad and draws a stick figure drawing of a woman with large boobs.

"There," she says. "Sign that and turn it in."

Elias looks at it for a second and then shrugs. He writes his name and class number and follows her toward the front of the room where other students are turning in their drawings. As he waits, he notices a bloody hole in his long-sleeved shirt. He lifts the sleeve to see a large gash in the same place where the static figure stabbed him with its long pointed appendage.

Elias and Roe are eating lunch together in a buffet-style college cafeteria. The room is mostly empty but for a few tables of students. The sun shines through the window onto them. Everyone in the room is languid and rather quiet, like they are all suffering from bad hangovers. Roe has a giant plate of food—a slice of pizza, a stack of hamburger steaks, mashed potatoes smothered with chipped beef gravy, a miniature quiche, waffles covered in syrup, bacon, tacos, and a slice of chocolate pie. She eats only a tiny bit of everything. Elias, on the other hand, has a small plate of fruit and ham and toast and he's barely eating anything at all.

"Have you ever fallen asleep standing up?" Elias asks.

Roe dips her pizza in chipped beef gravy and takes a bite. She answers with food still in her mouth.

"Ummm… I don't think so," she says.

"I think I fell asleep while standing in class today. Last night as well."

Roe is barely listening, focusing more on her food. She takes a bottle of hot sauce from the side of the table and dumps it all over her hamburger steaks and then eats them with a fork and knife like a stack of pancakes.

"I had these really weird dreams," Elias says. "They felt real. *Really* real. And when I woke up I felt even more exhausted than when I went to sleep."

Roe wipes a giant glob of hot sauce off of her face and creates a pile of wadded-up napkins on the table next to her plate.

"That's kind of nuts," she says. "I didn't even know it was possible to fall asleep on your feet."

He pulls up his sleeve to show a red mark on his wrist. "I also have this cut on my arm that I swear—"

Elias is interrupted by a loud slam on the table as Jake drops his tray of food next to him.

"What's up, doucheboners?" Jake says.

He takes his seat next to Elias and shoves him to the side so that he can sit directly across from Roe. When Roe sees Jake, she rolls her eyes, not in the least bit excited to see him.

"Where's the party tonight?" Jake asks.

Roe shrugs. "There's a kegger tomorrow in Alpine Heights. No word about tonight."

"Well, if nothing's going on elsewhere we'll make our own party," Jake says.

"I'm not going to just drink in your room with your stupid friends again," Roe says.

"Then we'll get a keg. Fifth floor party."

Roe shakes her head. "I don't know. That's just asking for trouble."

"The RA is a total stoner. He won't give a shit."

"I'm not talking about the RA. I'm talking about being the only woman in a hall full of drunken screeps. The dorm seems like it's full of assholes this year."

Jake shrugs. "Then go to the women's dorm and invite some girls over."

"Fuck that. I'm not bringing any girls to a party at Crestridge Dorm. I don't want to be responsible if any of them get roofied."

"Nobody's ever been roofied at Crestridge Dorm. Those are just rumors."

"Bullshit," Roe says.

"Nobody I've ever hung out with would do anything like that."

"Are you kidding? Your boy Mikel is the main screep I'm talking about."

"Mikel's not a screep," Jake says.

"Are you kidding?" Roe says. "Mikel's the biggest screep on campus. I bet he's got roofies on him right now. And you're a screep, too."

"Why am I a screep?" Jake asks.

Elias looks at them with a confused face.

"What's a screep?" he asks.

The other two glare at him like they had forgotten he was sitting there with them.

"A screep is a sketchy creep," Roe explains. "The kind of guy that makes women uncomfortable to be around. Whatever you do in this school, don't turn into a screep."

"Yeah, if women think you're a screep then you'll never get laid," Jake says.

"That right there," Roe says, pointing at Jake. "What you just said. That's what makes you a screep."

"What?" Jake holds up his hands. "I was just agreeing with you…"

"Fucking racist…" Roe says.

Jake shakes his head, not sure what he did wrong. Elias can't help but laugh at the exchange. But when Jake gives him a dirty look, Elias just lowers his head and returns to eating his lunch.

CHAPTER
FOUR

Roe is standing in front of the dorm room sink, applying makeup in the mirror. She's wearing dance club attire—skinny jeans and a small red tank top that reveals a dangling navel piercing and the lower section of a tattoo on her abdomen. Elias lies on his bed, playing an old J-RPG game on his tablet. Bass is pumping in the background from somebody blasting hiphop in a distant dorm room.

Roe looks at him through the reflection in the mirror.

"You should get in the shower," she says. "We're leaving at 8."

Elias lowers his tablet.

"I don't think I want to go to a party tonight," he says.

"We're not going to a party," she says. "We decided to go to the club instead."

"A dance club?"

Roe pauses to apply vampyr-plum lipstick to her lips.

"Yeah, you dance don't you?"

Elias shrugs. "Not really."

"If you're worried that no girl will dance with you, don't sweat it. I'll hook you up."

"Thanks, but I'm just tired. I feel like I didn't sleep at all last night."

"Just take a shower. It'll wake you up."

"I don't know…" Elias says, shrinking deeper into his bed.

"Come on, you'll have fun."

Roe sits on her bed and squeezes into a pair of heeled acrylic boots that go all the way to her knees. She laces them up tight, leaning back so that her leg is straight in the air. Elias watches her intently.

"Just get in the shower and see how you feel," she tells him.

Elias is in a dingy shower stall coated in mildew. Half the tiles on the floor and wall are either cracked or missing completely. Graffiti is all over the walls around him. He is still wearing his clothes with a towel over his shoulder, trying to close the dirt-caked curtain behind him. Half of the curtain has been ripped off the rings and dangles to the side. He lets out a sigh when he realizes he can only close it halfway. He drapes his towel over the bar to cover the open space, spreading it out as much as he can. Then he takes off his clothes and drapes them over the towel one piece at a time.

He turns on the shower and only a small trickle of water comes out. He adjusts the rusty decades-old metal knobs but it doesn't change the water flow. He pokes his head under the small stream and moans in frustration. Then he soaps himself up and puts shampoo in his hair, trying to make do with the little water he has.

A group of three drunk guys dressed like complete douchebags bursts into the bathroom, hooting and hollering. Their voices echo loudly but their words are not intelligible to Elias. Two of them stop at the urinals and piss like racehorses. One of them goes to a mirror closest to Elias. As the drunk guy combs his hair in the mirror, checking himself out, he catches sight of Elias through the opening in the shower stall. When he sees Elias, he smirks. Then turns to his friends.

"Hey, somebody's in the shit shower."

His two friends look over at him and then in unison, they flush the urinals. As the water becomes piping hot in the shower, Elias cries out.

"Oh fuck!"

The three guys burst into laughter.

"Serves you right, racist!" says the drunk guy closest to him.

He rips Elias' towel and clothes off of the shower rod and the three of them run out of the bathroom, laughing.

Elias stands there in shock, shampoo running into his eyes. He stands off to the side so that nobody can see him through the opening in the shower curtain, even though he's by himself.

"I'm not a racist…"

Elias steps out of the bathroom and looks around to see if anybody is watching. Then he runs out, covering his crotch with his hands. He sees his towel down the hall and races for it. He wraps it around his waist. Then he goes for the rest of his clothes scattered down the hallway. Before he can get to his underwear, two girls step out of a dorm room with their two boyfriends. As they pass Elias, he tries to act casually as he picks up his boxer briefs. Once they are in the stairwell, he frantically pulls on his underwear beneath the towel.

Elias bursts into his dorm room, struggling to get his shirt on. As he enters, his towel drops to the floor exposing his underwear. His face goes red with embarrassment. But when he looks around the room, he finds himself all alone. He sighs with relief and closes the door behind him. As he pulls on his pants, he notices a note on the mirror. He goes to it and pulls it off.

It reads:

WE WENT TO THE CLUB. MEET
US THERE.
—ROE

Elias turns the paper over but there isn't anything written on the other side.

"Which club?"

Elias drops the note and goes to his bed and lies down. Just as he gets comfortable, somebody bursts into his room. He turns to see Mikel in the doorway.

He says, "Hey, bro. Where's Roe at?"

He steps inside and makes himself at home.

"She went to the club," Elias responds.

Mikel goes to the fridge and pulls out one of Roe's beers. He cracks it open and takes a swig. "Which club?"

Elias sits up. "I don't know. She didn't say."

"Did Jake go with her?"

"I don't know. Probably."

"Those fuckers ditched me? What a bunch of racists."

Elias looks at him with a confused face.

"Why does everyone call each other racists here?" he asks.

Mikel takes another swig of beer and shrugs. "I don't know. It's like calling somebody an asshole… but worse."

Something catches Mikel's attention and his eyes light up.

"Oh shit!" he says.

He goes to Roe's side of the room and picks up a pair of panties amongst the dirty clothes scattered on the floor.

"Roe's underwear! Did she wear these?"

He holds them up like a sacred treasure, stretching out the nylon elastic.

"Dude, put those back," Elias says.

He presses the black panties to his face, inhaling their scent. Elias gets to his feet and rushes to him.

"Don't be a creep," he says.

When Elias goes to grab the underwear, Mikel pulls back, holding them away.

"You just want them for yourself," Mikel says. "You're

probably smelling her underwear every time she leaves the room."

"I don't smell her underwear," Elias says, a look of disgust on his face.

"Sure you don't."

Mikel runs backs into the hallway. Elias doesn't follow him. Mikel holds up the pair of panties in triumph.

"I'm keeping these," he says.

He stuffs them into his pocket and walks away. Elias goes into the hall and watches him walk off, then closes the door and locks it. He lets out a sigh.

"Racist."

Elias is asleep in his bed, wearing his sleeping attire—a shirt and sweatpants. Party music is blasting from some room in the distance. The sound of drunk students running and shouting through the hallway outside his door wakes him up. He turns over and looks at the time on the microwave above the minifridge. It reads 2:33 am. He looks over at Roe's bed, but it's empty. He turns over and goes back to sleep.

Elias wakes up a couple hours later to somebody hovering over him. He opens his eyes and looks up to see Roe. She is stripped down to her bra and underwear, leaning close to his face.

She whispers to him, "Hey, Eliot… Wake up. I'm bored."

She pulls open his covers and crawls into bed with him.

"Wait… what are you doing?"

"I just want to have some fun," she says.

She gets on top of him and puts her hands on his shoulders, looking him directly in the eyes.

"You're drunk," Elias says.

She giggles drunkenly.

"I'm not drunk," she says. "I only drank a little drenium and mykalits."

Elias looks confused by her answer. "What?"

"Jeshua gave me some at the skate park," she explains.

"Skate park? I thought you went dancing."

Roe giggles at him.

"Stop talking," she says. "You're being annoying."

She puts her fingers on his lips. Long claw-like fingernails dig into his nose as she leans in and kisses his neck.

"Wait." He pushes her back. "We're roommates. We shouldn't do this."

"Do what?" she asks in an annoyed tone.

Elias pauses for a moment.

"We shouldn't sleep together," he says.

She laughs in his face.

"Oh, Eliot…" she says. "You're so cute. Are you a virgin?"

"Um… No…" he says.

"Don't be shy…"

Elias looks over her shoulder and realizes something odd about the room. Old sheets are hanging from the ceiling. Broken wooden furniture covered in cobwebs litters the room where their desks used to be.

"Besides, I don't want to sleep with you…" she says.

Elias looks her in the eyes and sees that her face has

changed. Goat horns are growing out of the sides of her head. Her eyes are pools of black. Her skin is white and cracked, almost like it's made of porcelain.

"I want to eat you," she says.

She opens her mouth to reveal a row of sharpened teeth.

"You don't mind, do you?" she asks.

"What the hell are you talking about?" he cries.

Elias tries to get away, but she holds him down. Then she lunges at him and bites into his shoulder, snarling like an animal. As he struggles, she pushes him down with all of her weight and digs her teeth deeper into his flesh. With all his strength, he's able to pry her mouth from his shoulder, a chunk of meat coming off in her teeth.

She leans back, chewing his flesh like it's the most delicious thing in the world, and then swallows. Elias stares up at her in horror. As panic stretches across Elias' face, Roe lifts her arms and looks down at her body. Her porcelain skin is cracking and crumbling, dropping from her body in tiny chunks.

"Oh, shit…" she says, touching her body. "I'm falling to pieces."

Elias whimpers beneath her as flakes of skin pile onto his chest.

She says, "Quick, let me eat more of you before I crumble to nothing."

Roe wraps her crumbling arms around him and sinks her teeth into his neck.

CHAPTER
FIVE

Elias cries out and sits up in bed. He's back in his normal room. The morning sun is shining through the window. He looks over at Roe who is lying on her bed. She's on top of her blankets, still dressed how she was the night before. She didn't even bother taking off her boots.

She looks over at him.

"What's wrong?" she asks.

Elias looks around, confused about what has happened. He takes a deep breath and then looks at Roe.

"Nothing," he says, trying to calm down. "I must have had a nightmare or something."

She laughs. "Seriously?"

Elias gets a glass of water from the side of his bed. His hand is shaking as he takes a sip.

"Must have been a bad one," she says.

Elias can't even look in her direction as he says, "Yeah…"

Elias gets out of bed and digs through his clothes in his dresser, still clearly shaking.

"I'm lucky," she says. "I never remember my dreams."

She sits up and removes her boots.

"Where were you last night?" she says. "I looked for you everywhere."

She pulls her blanket over her lower body and removes her pants beneath the covers.

Elias says, "You didn't tell me which club you went to in your note so I just went to bed early."

Roe pulls her pants out from under the blanket and tosses them onto the floor.

She thinks about it for a second and then says, "Oh, yeah... sorry about that."

Then she lies back into a comfortable position, her hand behind her head.

"Well, I'll make it up to you tonight. There's a kegger off campus. I promise we won't leave you behind."

Once Elias has his school clothes picked out, he drapes them over his arm.

"By the way," he says, "Mikel came in and stole a pair of your underwear last night. I couldn't stop him."

Roe gives him a look of disgust. "*What!* Are you serious?"

Elias nods.

"Ewww. What a screep. I'm going to kill his ass later."

Elias grabs his backpack and goes for the exit.

"Hey..." she says.

Elias looks back.

She gives him a nod of approval. "Thanks for telling me."

As he looks into her eyes, an image flashes into Eliot's mind of her looking like she did in his dream. It's the monstrous version of her with horns and porcelain skin.

64

He shakes his head and looks away and the vision vanishes.

"Are you bleeding?" she asks him.

Roe points at his shoulder.

"What?" He looks down at blood oozing through his shirt. "Oh shit..."

Then he rushes out of the room.

Elias is looking in the bathroom mirror at a bite mark on his neck. His shirt is coated in blood from his shoulder down to his stomach. There are red spots where sharpened teeth had broken the skin on his neck. He cringes as he peels back his shirt to reveal a much larger gaping wound on his shoulder. A large chunk of meat is missing. Blood is still trickling out of the wound when he puts pressure on the skin next to it. He touches it with his finger, winces at the pain and recoils.

"Fuck..."

Jake, Mikel and Gregory are passing by the open bathroom door when they see Elias looking in the mirror. Jake notices the wound and enters the bathroom.

"Whoa," he calls out. "What happened to you, bro?"

Mikel and Gregory follow him inside.

Mikel laughs when he sees the wound on Elias' shoulder. "Whoa, dude! You got fucked up."

They all come in for a closer look.

"It looks like he was mauled by an animal," Mikel says.

"I don't think it was an animal," Gregory says.

Mikel points at the wound. "Those are bite marks. Looks like a zombie got him."

Elias lets go of his shirt collar and turns to them. Jake comes closer and looks him straight in the eyes. A serious expression on his face.

"Hey," he says in a serious tone. "What happened?"

Elias just shakes his head. "I have no idea." He looks away and pauses. Then he says, "I had a weird dream last night. I dreamt that some strange woman crawled into bed with me and bit me on the neck. When I woke up, I was bleeding."

Elias doesn't want to tell him the truth. He doesn't want to say that it was Roe that did this or that she did it to him inside of some kind of dream.

Mikel bursts into laughter. "Oh shit, it was probably Roe. She does that kind of shit when she's drunk."

Mikel keeps laughing, but the other two guys have serious looks on their faces.

"I told you she's a freak!" Mikel says. "I don't know why you guys are so into her."

Jake shoves Mikel. "It wasn't Roe."

"Who else could it have been?" Mikel asks.

Jake says, "Don't you think he could be lying?"

Jake turns his attention to Elias.

Elias holds up his hands. "I'm not lying. That's what happened."

Jake asks, "You didn't try to do anything to Roe when she was sleeping last night, did you?"

Jake's posture becomes more aggressive. Elias becomes nervous.

"What do you mean?" Elias asks.

"I mean the only way Roe would bite you like that is if it was self-defense. Did you try to force yourself on her or something?"

"No," Elias says. "Never."

Mikel bounces up and down. "Oh shit! I knew this guy was a pervert!"

Elias cries, "I'm not a pervert. I swear."

Before Jake can get more aggressive, Gregory gets between them. "Come on. I think he's telling the truth."

Jake turns his attention to Gregory. "What? You think he really dreamed that?"

"No, but that doesn't mean he tried to assault her," Gregory says.

Jake stares down his friend, but Gregory just says, "Just ask Roe if you don't believe him."

Jake relaxes a bit and takes a step back. "Fine…" Jake puts on a pair of overly large hipster glasses with bright green frames in an intimidating manner as though they are cool-guy sunglasses and not completely ridiculous whatsoever. He points at Elias. "But if you tried anything with her, you're dead."

He charges out of the bathroom into the hallway. Mikel laughs and chases after him. Before Gregory leaves, he turns back to Elias.

"There's a hospital on campus," Gregory tells him. "You should get that checked out."

Elias nods. "Thanks."

After Gregory leaves, Elias grabs his pants from the ground and changes his clothes.

Elias sits at a desk in a dimly lit half-empty classroom, looking at his phone. There's a large bandage on his neck and shoulder. On the large projection screen, the philosophy teacher is sitting at a table, giving a lecture. It is the same teacher that he saw in all of his classes the day before.

The philosophy teacher says, "So philosophy is pretty much the most useless class you could possibly take in college. It really won't help you in the real world whatsoever. You'd be better off taking water polo or Greek mythology or eighteenth fucking century French literature. But hey, it's your money so knock yourselves out. At least it's not the history of Jpop nutrition that I taught last semester. Jesus Christ that was stupid."

While the teacher is speaking, Elias opens the text messages on his phone and sees a message from his mother.

The text message reads: Hey, I saw you charged $1.5 million to the emergency credit card this morning.

Elias texts his mother: Sorry about that. I had to go to the campus hospital.

MOM: Why? What happened?

MOM: Are you okay?

ELIAS: I'm fine. It was no big deal.

MOM: Well, why did you go to the hospital if it was no big deal? I can't afford to pay that kind of money.

ELIAS: I needed stitches.

MOM: Stitches for what? You weren't drinking and doing something stupid were you?

ELIAS: No, it happened in my sleep.
MOM: What's that supposed to mean?
ELIAS: I'll talk to you later. I'm in philosophy class.
MOM: Why are texting in class? Pay attention!
MOM: Love you.

She texts some heart emojis and Elias gives her message a thumbs up. Then he puts his phone away.

A keg party is raging at an off-campus building that is large enough to be a small frat house. Two stories plus a basement, at least six bedrooms. The perfect party house. Elias is waiting in the kitchen in the middle of a line for the keg forty people deep. He holds an empty plastic cup in his hand, uncomfortable in such a thick crowd that doesn't even give him any elbow room. Kpop boy band music is blasting and half the people are dancing to it. The other half are chugging beer and elbow-bumping. Most of the students are wearing multi-colored face masks pulled down to their chins. Only a few are covering their faces.

Roe comes up behind Elias and grabs him by the shoulders. She's wearing a baby blue t-shirt and the same skinny jeans she wore the night before.

"Hey, there you are," Roe says.

Elias is startled and awkward in her presence. "Oh, hi."

"You made it. Sorry Jake wouldn't let you ride with us. He's being a real asshole today."

Elias nods. "Yeah…"

Roe takes a swig of her beer from a plastic cup.

"Can I cut in line behind you?" she asks.

"Sure…" He points at her cup. "But don't you already have a full beer?"

"It'll be empty by the time we get up there," she says.

She cuts in line in front of him. She stands with her back to the line so that she can face him. When she sees the bandages on his neck and shoulder, she leans in closer.

"Oh, fuck! You really got messed up last night. What happened?" She pokes at his wound and he recoils.

"It happened in my sleep," Elias says. "The doctor said that he thinks a rat was gnawing on my neck."

"Ewww, gross! That's fucked up." She makes a cringing expression and shakes the thought from her head. "We're getting rat poison and traps tomorrow. I knew Crestridge Dorm was infested but I draw the line at rat bites. If I wake up to one of those things chewing on my face I'm going to burn the whole place to the ground."

Elias says, "The doctor said he's treated a lot of similar wounds from people in Crestridge Dorm over the past couple of years. He didn't know what they were, originally. Students would just wake up with strange wounds for no explainable reason."

Roe walks backward as they go farther up the line. "Yeah, stuff like that used to happen to my last roommate sometimes. He used to wake up with wounds all over his body. Cuts, bite marks, bruises. It was weird. I always thought he was doing it to himself. You know, to get attention. But maybe it was just rats."

"Maybe…"

"Jake thought I was the one who did that to you," Roe says. Then she laughs. "Can you believe it?"

"Yeah…"

"He's such an asshole. He's always trying to protect me from other guys. Not because he's a nice guy, but because he thinks I'll sleep with him for it. Like I owe him or something. I don't need anyone like that protecting me."

"Then why do you hang out with him?"

"Because he has a fake ID. I'll put up with his bullshit as long he can buy me beer."

Elias nods. They move farther up the line, almost to the front.

Roe says, "I used to have another friend on our floor who was twenty-one that I'd get my beer from. He was a good guy. Super chill. Way more chill than Jake."

"Why don't you get beer from him instead?" Elias asks.

"Can't. He dropped out last semester. It was weird, too. He was just about to graduate, but took off out of nowhere."

They get to the front of the line. Roe chugs the rest of her beer. Then she pumps the keg and refills her cup.

"I kind of think it was my fault. He took off right after we slept together for the first time. It wouldn't be the first time a guy left town after sleeping with me, but still…"

Roe finishes filling her beer and moves the tap to Elias' cup, filling it up for him. Elias lifts his cup to give her a better angle.

Elias says, "Wait, are you saying he disappeared right after—"

Halfway through the pour, foam and air shoot from the tap, interrupting Elias' sentence.

"Oh, shit," Roe says. "The keg's tapped."

She drops the tap. Elias looks at his cup of foam. Roe turns to the massive line behind them and yells, "Keg's tapped, everyone!"

The partygoers all groan and shout in disappointment. A black male college student with long dreadlocks who was waiting in line behind Elias steps closer and says, "What the fuck? I've been waiting for an hour."

"It's not my fault," Roe says.

"Bullshit. You cut in line. Give me some of your beer." The student reaches out for her cup, but she pulls it away.

"Kill yourself, racist," Roe tells him.

The black guy looks at her with an annoyed expression. "Did you just call me a racist?"

Roe gets awkward for a moment. "Uh, you know what I mean…"

Then she rushes out of the kitchen.

Elias follows Roe into the living room, sipping on his cup of foam. They enter a crowded dance floor filled with sweaty students, swaying to the thumping beat. Roe weaves her way through the throngs of people and joins Jake and Mikel, who are attempting to impress two disinterested girls. When Roe interrupts, the two girls take the opportunity to flee. She leans in close to Jake to speak over the blaring music.

"The keg's tapped," she tells him.

"Already?" Jake asks.

"You need to go on a beer run."

Jake gets annoyed. "They charged twenty grand for these cups."

"Let's just get our own beer," she says. "We'll stash it in your car."

"What do you want?" he asks.

Roe pulls out a wad of bills and hands it to Jake. "Quantity over quality. Get as much as you can."

Mikel dishes out some cash to add to the funds. Then they turn to Elias.

"Chip in," Jake says.

Elias pulls all the money out of his wallet. "I only have ten grand that's supposed to be for food for the rest of the week."

Jake grabs his money anyway. "Okay, I'll be back in a few minutes."

A new Kpop song comes on the speakers. When Roe hears it, her eyes light up.

"Oh, shit! This is my favorite song!" She turns to Elias. "Come on. Dance with me."

She turns to Jake. "Hold this."

She hands Jake her beer. Then takes off onto the dance floor. But before Elias can join her, Jake gets in front of him and gives him a serious look. "I want you to stay away from Roe."

Elias shoots him a confused look. "But she's my roommate."

"I don't give a fuck. I don't trust you."

Elias points at the bandage on his neck. "The doctor said these are rat bites. It wasn't Roe."

"Bullshit."

Jake turns to Mikel and hands him Roe's beer. "Watch him while I'm gone."

"Sure…" Mikel says.

Jake pushes his way through Elias, forcing him deeper into the crowd. Then he heads for the exit.

The crowd has pushed Elias out of the room into a hallway. He is backed against a wall, nursing his beer. He peers out into the living room, watching Roe as she dances. Roe looks like she's having the time of her life. She finds a group of girls who are also enthusiastic about the Kpop song playing and dances with them.

Feeling left out, Elias tries to step into the living room to join the dancing but is immediately shoved back into the hallway by a group of partiers heading toward the kitchen.

Elias scans the room until his eyes lock onto Mikel. He sees the douchebag putting something in Roe's beer that he's holding. Mikel looks around the room after he does it until his eyes catch Elias'. They stare at each other for a moment. Then a big smile appears on Mikel's face. He puts his fingers up to his mouth, indicating that Elias should keep quiet about it. Then looks away.

When the song ends, Roe goes over to Mikel to reclaim her beer and takes a swig. She looks around the room for Elias but doesn't see him. Then she returns to the dance floor.

Elias panics as he squeezes his way into the living room toward Roe. He tries to get her attention.

"Roe!" he cries out, but his voice can't be heard over the music.

Roe continues dancing.

"Roe! Don't drink your beer!"

He tries shoving his way through the crowd, but it becomes too dense. He grabs the shoulder of a male student with a red baseball cap.

"Let me through," Elias tells him.

But the student with a red baseball cap shoves him. "Kill yourself."

Elias keeps moving. Squeezing his way through one person at a time. He looks around, but he's lost sight of Roe. When he finally gets to the dance floor, Roe is no longer there. He looks around the room but neither Mikel nor Roe is anywhere to be seen. He moves on.

Elias steps outside in a panic, scanning the porch for Roe. There's a group of college girls sitting on the steps vaping and chatting. Elias goes to them.

He asks, "Hey, did a girl come out here? Black hair, bangs. Blue shirt."

One of them looks over at him and flips him off.

"Get lost, screep," she tells him.

Then the girls laugh at him.

Elias scans the area. He tosses his beer on the ground

in frustration. "Fuck!"

Then he goes back inside.

Across the party, Elias catches sight of Roe and Mikel. She is limp and staggering. Mikel is helping her up the stairs, laughing and waving off anyone who tries to help.

Elias shoves his way through the crowd but quickly loses sight of Roe. He pushes even harder, racing toward the stairs. He knocks over a drunk girl's drink as he pushes through.

The girl yells, "What the fuck, asshole!"

Elias keeps moving.

Behind him, the drunk girl's boyfriend steps forward. He's a shirtless, tall, muscled guy wearing only jeans. He widens his arms in an intimidating posture.

"You wanna go, bro!" he yells.

Elias ignores him and continues toward the stairs.

Elias gets to the top of the stairs and searches for Roe among the people crowding the hallway. He goes to the closest room and finds a group of stoners passing a bong around. He goes to another door and opens it to a couple of girls making out while three guys watch from the floor, cheering them on. They give Elias an annoyed look, he closes the door and moves on.

When he gets to the last door on the floor, he tries the knob but the door is locked. He pounds his fist on the door.

"Roe? Are you in there?"

He knocks again. There's no answer. He pauses, catching his breath. He looks around.

"Fuck it."

He kicks the door. Putting all of his weight on it. He kicks three more times until the door opens.

Elias falls into the bedroom as he breaks through the lock. He looks up to see Roe lying half-conscious on the bed, her jeans pulled down to her knees. Mikel is standing there with his shirt off.

"What the fuck, bro?" Mikel says. "Get out of here. Can't you see I'm busy?"

Elias is agitated. He straightens himself up and points at Mikel. "Get away from her!"

Mikel snickers. A creepy smile stretches across his face. "Come on, bro. Don't be a cock-block."

Roe tries to sit up. "What's going on you guys?"

Then she falls back down.

"You roofied her!" Elias yells.

"You can have your turn after I'm done. Just watch the door for me."

"Fuck that. If you lay a hand on her, I'll…"

Mikel gets in his face, flexing at him. "You'll what?"

Elias steps back and pulls out his phone.

"I'll call the cops," he says.

As Elias starts dialing, Mikel lunges at him. He grabs the phone.

"You're not calling shit."

As they struggle for the phone, Roe goes limp on the bed and falls into unconsciousness. Mikel drops the phone as his body starts to disintegrate into a swirling mist of purplish-gray. Elias watches the phone fall to the ground as the same transformation happens to him. His skin becomes ethereal, his bones dissolve into vapor, and he feels his entire body losing its physical form.

Mikel looks at Elias with panic in his eyes. "Hey, what the hell's going on, bro?"

Elias is in just as much shock and confusion as Mikel.

"It's happening to you, too?" he asks.

They step away from each other as they dissolve into ghostly specters.

Mikel cries, "What is this? What's happening to me?"

The vapor that used to be Mikel and Elias forms misty tendrils that drift toward Roe's mouth. She inhales them in one long stream, swallows, and lets out a sigh.

CHAPTER
SIX

Elias and Mikel materialize in the center of the dance floor of the party house, only it is darker and dingier than it was before. The walls are cracked and covered in blood-red vines. Warped music plays on what sounds like a melted record in the background. They are surrounded by faceless mannequin-like people that dance slowly around them. The mannequin people are wearing gray rags as dresses or wrapped around them like togas. Some have smooth bald heads while others wear wigs.

Mikel looks around in a panic. "Where the hell are we?"

Elias is a little more composed than Mikel. He steps away from a mannequin woman as she dances behind him with stiff movements.

"I don't know. I think it's just a dream."

They stand back-to-back, facing the mannequins dancing around them.

"How the fuck is this a dream?" Mikel asks.

"It's happened to me before."

Mikel pushes a male mannequin that dances too

close to him. "How is this a dream if we're both in it?"

"It's not our dream," Elias says.

Roe appears in the stairwell upstairs. She's wearing a long black sleeveless wedding dress. She has the same crumbling porcelain skin as she did the night before, the same goat horns growing from her head. But her eyes are much larger and bug out of her head. They are the big black bulbous eyes of a wasp or a bee. A noose is around her neck, but the rope stretches far behind her and doesn't appear to have an end.

"Eliot, you're back," she says.

A smile appears on her face. She steps down the staircase. The noose and her long dress trail behind her.

"Have you come to dance with me?" she asks.

Mikel becomes uneasy when he sees Roe. "Who the fuck is that? Is that Roe?"

Elias nods his head. "Yeah."

"Why does she look like that? What's wrong with her?"

"This is what she's like in her dreams," Elias says.

As Roe gets to the bottom of the stairs, she pulls out a long razor-sharp knife. The two men back up a few steps when they see the weapon.

"I love dancing," she says.

As Roe steps toward the dance floor, several mannequin people dance across her path. She stabs the closest one in the chest twice. Dark gray blood gushes out of the mannequin and sprays across the dance floor. Then she slashes at two others, cutting her way toward Elias and Mikel.

As she gets closer, Roe's eyes connect with Mikel's.

"Eliot, you brought a friend." A smile stretches across her face.

She steps closer to Mikel.

"Hey, I know you," she says. "You're Mitchel."

Mikel backs away. "Stay the fuck away from me, you freak."

Roe's smile drops from her face. She turns to Elias. "I don't like your friend, Eliot." The expression on her face turns to disgust. "He's very rude."

She raises her knife and points it at Mikel.

"He needs to show me respect," she says.

Mikel digs into the sheath strapped to his waist, hidden beneath his shirt, and pulls out three throwing knives. He holds one up and points it at her.

"Stay back, bitch."

Roe continues to move forward. Elias gets behind Mikel, using him as cover.

"You brought knives with you to a party?" Elias asks.

Mikel ignores the question.

"Tell your psycho girlfriend to get away from me."

"She's not my girlfriend," Elias says.

Roe turns to Elias and makes a faux-disappointed expression.

"Awwww. Eliot, why don't you want me to be your girlfriend? I thought we were getting along so well."

Roe grabs another dancing mannequin woman and cuts her throat. Gray blood gushes down her pale body as she writhes in Roe's arms.

"You could at least give me one dance," Roe says.

Mikel throws one of his knives at Roe and it sticks into

81

her shoulder. She looks at Mikel with a distressed face.

"Oww. That hurt, Mitchel!"

Mikel throws another knife, but Roe uses the mannequin body she's holding as a shield. She frowns in a cutesy manner.

"You're so mean!" Roe cries, giving him a pouty face.

She charges forward, holding the dead mannequin woman in front of her. Mikel panics and throws his last knife in a sloppy manner that bounces off the mannequin.

"Run!" Mikel cries.

Mikel shoves his way past the dancers, heading for the front door. Elias follows him.

Roe drops the mannequin. "Wait. Don't go."

Elias' feet get tangled in the legs of a group of dancers and he falls over.

Mikel keeps running. He gets to the door and slams into it. He tries grabbing the knob but his hand can't grip it. The door is just painted onto the face of the wall. He flattens the palms of his hands against the door painting, feeling it out.

"It's not real…" he cries.

Mikel goes to the window. There is nothing but blackness on the other side. He tries to open it but it won't budge, so he steps back and tries kicking it.

"None of this is fucking real!"

He kicks the glass twice, but it's as hard as stone. On the third attempt, his foot breaks through the glass. The window comes alive. It grows angry eyes in the frame. The shattered glass becomes jagged teeth. Mikel's eyes light up in fear as the glass teeth close violently around the calf of his leg and bite it off. Blood sprays across the window and Mikel falls to the ground, screaming at the top of his lungs.

"Motherfucker!"

Roe walks casually past Elias toward Mikel, picking at the edge of her knife with her long fingernails. When she gets to the other side of the dance floor, her noose stops her in her tracks, tugging on her neck. She cuts the rope off at her chest and continues moving on.

Mikel squirms on the ground, pulling himself across the floor on his back, trying to get away from the window as his shredded stump of a leg oozes blood across the floor.

Roe goes to him. She steps casually to his front in order to face him, looking down on his sorry state with a faux-sympathetic look.

"Oh Mitchel, you look so pathetic when you're in pain."

Mikel struggles to move across the floor.

"Get the fuck away from me!" he cries.

"You're my guest. I just want to help you feel more comfortable."

She steps her leg over him and lowers herself onto his stomach, covering half his body with her flowing black dress. As she leans in toward Mikel, he punches her in the face, right in the left eye.

"Fucking bitch!" he yells.

Roe recoils a little, holding her hand to her eye.

"Oww. Why are such a jerk?" She puts the blade of her knife to his neck. "I'm just trying to cut your head off."

Then she pushes on the blade using both hands,

putting all of her weight into it.

Elias holds out his hand. "Don't!"

Mikel screams and thrashes as the blade cuts through his neck. Blood spurts out of the wound and covers the woman's face and dress. Roe moans in pleasure as the blade cuts through his neck. Mikel's voice goes quiet as the blade goes through his throat. He becomes limp. The blade makes a loud clanking noise as it hits the tile floor, severing Mikel's head from his body.

Elias gets to his feet, facing Roe.

"You killed him."

Roe looks up at Elias and smiles. She stands up, covered in blood. She wipes her blade against the side of her dress.

"Don't worry, Eliot. Mitchel wasn't a very good friend for you anyway. You're much better off without him."

Roe steps toward Elias with her arms outstretched.

"Now we can dance without interruptions."

Elias looks around the room for a way out. As Roe approaches him, he steps back onto the dance floor. He finds himself trapped by the mannequin dancers encircling him. Roe enters the dance floor, her bug-like eyes locked onto his. Elias looks around like a trapped animal. He isn't able to find an escape route before she gets to him.

When she's within five feet, she holds her arms up in a dancing pose, gesturing him to come closer.

"Come to me," she says.

Elias doesn't move. He's shivering. His eyes darting around the room in a panic. As she steps closer, his eyes lock onto hers. She takes his hands and pulls one around her back, holding the other up with the knife.

"There you go," she says, taking a long breath to calm herself.

They dance gently in a circle to the warped music, stepping through pools of gray mannequin blood.

Elias breathes heavily, shaking uncomfortably. He's not able to look at her face as she stares at him with her insect-like eyes.

"Isn't this nice?" she asks.

She leads him as they dance, but he's too unnerved to follow properly.

"Just relax," she says. "This is supposed to be fun."

Elias looks at her. "You killed Mikel…"

She shakes her head. "Forget about him. He was an asshole. Just focus on the moment."

She closes in on him, wrapping her arms around his back and pulling him closer. She rests her head on his shoulder.

"This is nice…" she says, then kisses his cheek. "You're a nice one."

As they dance, Elias steps on Roe's flowing dress and she gets annoyed. She pulls back to look in his eyes, giving him an angry look.

"Don't step on my dress."

A meek expression appears on his face. "I'm sorry."

"Dance better," she says.

She embraces him again and they dance for another moment. But Elias whimpers. His breathing becomes rapid, like he's about to cry. Roe becomes even more annoyed.

"Stop being so nervous," she says. "You're ruining this."

"I'm sorry," Elias responds.

Roe pushes him back a little.

"Stop apologizing! What's wrong with you?"

She slashes him with her knife, cutting through his shirt.

"This is supposed to be romantic!" she cries.

Elias cowers, holding out his hands and pulling back his face. She continues slashing at him, cutting up his arms and hands.

"I'm sorry!"

"I just wanted to dance with you and you're being such a baby about it!" she says.

She stops waving her knife around and grabs him around the waist, pulling him close.

"Now shut up and kiss me."

Roe grabs him by the back of the head and pulls him toward her lips which grow larger and larger as they come toward his face.

CHAPTER
SEVEN

Elias is in the party house bedroom again. He steps backward, still thinking he's in Roe's grip. He waves his hands around, whimpering and shaking.

A group of partygoers are in the room with him, hovering around Roe. Jake is among them, patting Roe on the face. She's beginning to regain consciousness.

Jake calls out to her, "Roe? Wake up."

Roe's eyes flutter and look around with a confused expression at the people hovering over her.

She asks, "What's going on? What happened?"

A concerned girl holds Roe in a motherly manner, covering her exposed underwear with a blanket so that the men in the room can't see.

She asks, "Were you drugged? We think somebody drugged you."

Roe tries to sit up but is too woozy and falls back down.

Elias steps forward. "Is she okay?"

The others in the room turn to Elias, surprised to see him there like he appeared out of nowhere.

Jake stands up straight and approaches Elias.

"What the fuck did you do to her?" Jake asks him.

Elias tells him, "It wasn't me. It was Mikel. He put something in her beer."

"Bullshit." Jake points at the ripped-up state of Elias' shirt and the cuts on his arms. "What happened to you?"

Elias pauses to look down, surprised by his injuries. He holds out his arms, trying to come up with an explanation.

"Mikel did it," he says, not very comfortable with lying to them. "I tried to stop him from hurting Roe and we got into a fight."

Jake doesn't believe him. "With what? Did he have a butcher knife or something?"

Elias shakes his head. "No, he had…"

Roe cries out in pain, gripping at her shoulder. "Oh, fuck…"

Roe pulls down her shirt to reveal a small throwing knife embedded in her skin. Blood trickles from the wound.

The concerned girl gets to her feet and pulls out her phone. "I'm calling the police."

As the girl dials 9-11 and moves to the hallway, Jake goes to Roe. He examines the knife in her shoulder.

"It's Mikel's," he says. "One of his stupid throwing knives." Jake clenches his fists. "That motherfucker. I'm going to kill his ass."

Jake shoves Elias out of the way and charges toward the hallway.

"He's already dead…" Elias says, but he speaks so quietly that nobody hears him.

As Roe sits there gripping at the knife in her shoulder, Elias' eyes meet hers. They stare at each other for a moment. He almost tears up at the sight of her.

Roe has bandages over the wound where the knife was removed. She is looking in the mirror at her bruised and blackened left eye, trying to apply makeup to cover it up. But it's so swollen that no makeup will do enough to hide it. She sighs in frustration.

"I'm going to murder that asshole," she says.

Jake and Elias are in the room with her. Jake is on the couch, messing around on his phone with a disturbed expression on his face. Elias is sitting on his bed, watching Roe and twitching with anxiety.

"The police are looking for Mikel now," Jake says. "They'll find him. That asshole won't get away with this."

"He's *your* friend," Roe says.

Jake shakes his head. "Not anymore. I'll kill his ass if I see him again."

She says, "Well, if you never gave him my beer this wouldn't have happened."

"How the hell would I have known he would do that?" Jake yells.

"You knew I didn't trust him," she says.

"Well, I wasn't going to give it to your creepy roommate." Jake glances over at Elias with a sneer.

Roe goes to him and points in his face. "Hey, he

89

fought to protect me while I was unconscious and got all cut up in the process." She gestures to Elias' arms which are all stitched up and bandaged. "I might've been raped if it wasn't for him. Where the fuck were you?"

"I was buying you beer," Jake says.

"Well, you should have been watching your creepy-ass friend."

Jake stands up. "Fuck this. I don't need your abuse."

He walks out of the room. Roe slams the door behind him.

"What an asshole!" she yells.

She screams in frustration, then turns to Elias.

"Don't you have a class to go to?" she asks.

Elias goes for his backpack. "Yeah, I'll leave."

He heads for the door, but Roe blocks his path.

"No, stay," she says. "I don't want to be alone."

Elias sits back down. "Okay, sure… I'll stay."

Roe sits on the bed next to him.

"You think you know someone…" she says.

She puts her hands in her face, about to cry. Elias holds out his hand as if to hug her, but he hesitates and puts his hands down.

"I'm sorry…" he says.

Roe rubs tears from her cheeks and lowers her hands. "It's not your fault. You did all you could…"

She lays her head in his lap.

Elias backs up a little at first, awkward with her touching him. But then he lets it happen. He places his hand on her shoulder, then shivers with anxiety.

Elias is in a bathroom stall, sitting on the toilet with his clothes on. He pulls out his phone to find a message from his mother.

It reads: I saw another million dollars charged to the credit card from the hospital. Is everything alright?

Elias types in his phone: I'm fine. I got in a fight and needed more stitches.

He waits for a response.

Another message comes in: Are you serious? What happened?

He types: I was trying to help a girl who was almost molested by a guy in my dorm.

After a moment, a new message appears: What the hell's going on at that school of yours? Are you okay?

He responds: I don't know.

Then Elias puts his phone in his pocket and lets out a sigh.

He gets up and leaves the stall, then comes face to face with Gregory who was standing in the bathroom as though waiting for him. Gregory has a serious expression on his face.

"We need to talk," he says.

"What?" Elias asks.

"Come with me."

"Why?"

Gregory just turns and walks out of the bathroom. Elias follows him.

Gregory's dorm room walls are lined with shelves containing hundreds of volumes of manga and anime figurines. There's only one bed in the room, indicating he lives there alone. When Elias enters the room, Gregory closes the door behind them.

"Why'd you want to talk?" Elias asks.

Gregory pulls a handful of Japanese candy from a basket on his coffee table. He offers one to Elias.

"Kit Kat?" Gregory asks.

Elias takes the candy. He unwraps it and takes a bite. The taste makes him cringe with disgust.

"It's cucumber vinegar flavor. I have a subscription from Japan."

Elias sets the candy aside. "What's this all about?"

Gregory gestures to the small couch on the other side of the coffee table. "Have a seat."

Elias sits on the couch.

"I want to talk to you about Roe," he says.

Elias becomes uneasy. "What about her?"

"You've noticed something weird about her, haven't you?" he asks.

Elias pauses and stares at him for a moment. "What do you mean?"

Gregory explains, "Mikel never left the party last night, did he? The cops aren't going to find him because there's nothing to find. He just vanished."

"How do you know that?" Elias asks.

"It's happened dozens of times before," Gregory

says. "People who get close to Roe disappear and never come back. All of her roommates. All of her boyfriends. Even her parents and foster parents. Anyone who comes into her life ends up vanishing without a trace. They leave their belongings behind and nobody knows what's happened to them."

Elias stares at him. His hands tremble.

Gregory continues, "You're her roommate so you know what's going on with her, don't you? You've been brought into her dreams."

"You know about that?" Elias asks.

Gregory nods. "It happened to me once last year when she passed out in my room. One moment I'm digging through my fridge for a beer and the next thing I know I'm in a strange place with two other guys that lived on our floor. Not sure how to explain what happened but we were transported to some abandoned, dilapidated city that was being pummeled by tsunamis. Roe was there, on a rooftop. It was almost like she was commanding the waves, like she had power over them and wanted to destroy all the buildings we were hiding in. One of my friends was washed away. The other one had a mental breakdown. We fought for our lives and somehow pulled through. When Roe woke up, two of us were back in my dorm room but the third was never heard from again. I had no idea what happened to me at the time. It seemed like a crazy dream. The other survivor dropped out of school, but I kept a close eye on Roe ever since. I saw all of her roommates disappear, all of her boyfriends. I don't know what's going on with that girl but she's dangerous.

I wouldn't live with her if I were you."

Elias is unnerved by his words. "Why didn't you tell me sooner? You have no idea what I've been going through."

"Would you have believed me? Roe's other roommates didn't. I was waiting until I knew for sure you experienced what I'm talking about."

"So what do I do?" Elias asks.

"If I were you, I'd just drop out. Go back home."

Elias shakes his head. "I can't do that. My mom is paying a fortune for this school."

"Then switch dorm rooms," Gregory says.

"Roe says it's impossible to change dorms."

"Then find somewhere else to sleep. Or sleep in your dorm during the day and find somewhere else to spend your nights. You can even stay in my room sometimes, if you need to. Whatever you do, stay away from Roe as much as you can."

Elias thinks about it for a moment. Then he says, "I guess I can do that..."

Elias stands up. Before he can get to the door, Gregory grabs him and gives him a big awkwardly long hug.

"Stay safe, man. I'm rooting for you."

Gregory continues his awkward hug, rocking him back and forth.

"Thanks..." Elias says.

He just waits there for the large man to let him go, but Gregory only hugs tighter and pats him on the head like a concerned father.

Roe is sitting on her bed, wearing pajamas and playing with her phone. Elias is across from her in his bed, fully dressed. He's holding his tablet, but his attention is more focused on her, watching her like a hawk just in case she falls asleep.

"There's a protest on campus after class tomorrow," Roe says. "You want to go with me?"

"I thought protesting wasn't allowed on campus?"

Roe shrugs. "It's not. That's what the protest is about."

"Okay. Yeah, sure."

"Cool," she says. "Everyone should be there. Maybe we'll actually make some changes at this shitty school."

"Yeah…"

They sit on their separate beds for a while, playing with their electronic devices. Roe moans a few times as she reads social media. Elias looks up at her each time she moans, but doesn't ask her about it.

"I think I'm going to go to sleep early," Roe says. "I don't feel like drinking tonight. Do you mind if I turn off the lights?"

A look of panic stretches across Elias' face. "Yeah, go ahead."

Roe gets up and turns off all the lights in the room, then she lies back down and turns off the light next to her bed.

"Goodnight," she says.

She wraps herself up in her blanket and rolls over on her side. In the darkness with only his tablet to light up the room, Elias quivers with anxiety. Then he gets to his feet.

"I'll leave you alone so you can sleep," he says.

Roe just grunts a response. Then Elias leaves the room, taking his tablet and a pillow with him.

Elias is sitting in a men's bathroom stall, trying to sleep while on the toilet. He has the pillow on the side of the divider, resting his head on it. But he can't get comfortable. After a moment, he gives up and places the pillow on his lap. He pulls out his phone. There's a message from his mother.

His mom's text reads: You didn't respond to my last message. Is everything okay? Are you mad at me?

Elias types: Sorry. I'm fine.

He waits for a moment but doesn't get a response.

Then he types: Actually, things aren't fine. It's not working out for me here. Would it be okay with you if I came back home? Just for a semester. I'll come back in the spring if I can get a different dorm assignment.

Before he sends the message, Elias stares at it, takes a breath, and reads it over. Then he deletes the whole thing. He waits awhile but his mother never responds. He puts away his phone and returns his pillow to the divider to lay his head against it and tries to go to sleep.

CHAPTER
EIGHT

Elias is in a crowd of protesters in the center of campus. People are holding signs like "fix our school" and "students have rights." There are hundreds of college students chanting and jeering, but many people in the crowd aren't taking it very seriously. Some are treating it like a party, carrying around eighteen packs of beer and drinking openly. Jake is one of these people. He wears a helmet made of Natty Ice boxes as well as a cardboard Natty Ice chest plate covering his front and back like he's a champion knight for cheap beer. He chugs a can and throws the empty into the crowd in front of him. Gregory and Roe are also sipping on beers as they join in the "fix our school" chant. Elias is the only one not drinking, standing off to the side with his hands in his pockets.

A female voice comes on the intercom system, broadcasting across campus. The voice announces: "Attention all students. This is a protest-free zone. Participation or organization of political activism on campus may result in expulsion or possible incarceration."

The crowd reacts to the intercom voice, shouting

and jeering in protest. Jake and Roe are especially riled up when they hear it.

Jake yells, "Everett University is bullshit!"

Roe calls out, "Give us real classes!"

Jake cries, "This place is too expensive!"

Roe yells, "Let me into the women's dorm!"

When they finish chanting, Roe and Jake clink their beer cans and take a chug. They are not taking the protest too seriously, just having fun with being in such a large group of people. While Roe and Jake are engaged in the protest, Gregory goes to Elias and pats him on the shoulder.

"Are you okay, man?" he asks. "How'd it go last night?"

Elias shrugs. "It was fine. I slept in the bathroom."

"You could have crashed on my floor if you wanted."

Elias waves his words away. "No, I'm good. I was thinking I might go home for a while and come back next semester."

Gregory nods. "That's a good idea. I'm sure you'll get a new room assignment if you leave and come back."

Elias lets out a sigh and then says, "I just don't know what to say to my mom. She was planning on renting out my room at home. With the economy the way it is, she needs the money."

"Don't worry about that," Gregory says. "I'm sure she'd prefer you survive than have the extra cash."

Elias shakes his head. "She won't understand. She's working three jobs as it is."

"It'll be fine," Gregory says. "Anything's better than a life with her."

They both look at Roe who is chugging a beer with Jake. When they finish drinking, Roe and Jake spit a stream of beer onto the crowd in front of them and laugh. Elias takes an extra long time looking at Roe. There is a yearning in his eyes.

"Yeah, I guess…" he says.

A row of security guards appears in front of the crowd. They wear black riot gear that seems more like armor, shields, and batons. They all have MR-15 machine guns strapped to their waists, staring down the crowd like they aren't fucking around.

The presence of the armed guards only riles up the crowd even more. They throw empty beer cans and garbage at them, yelling and pointing. Roe and Jake get into the spirit of things and move closer to the security guards, spitting and yelling in their direction. The security guards move forward a few steps, showing the students that they won't be intimidated.

"It's starting to get rough," Gregory says. "We should get out of here."

Elias looks at Roe getting too close to the front line. A look of concern on his face.

"Nah, I'm going to stay," he says.

Despite his nervous posture, Gregory stays put. He takes a couple steps back, as though getting ready to run at any moment.

The female intercom voice comes back on: "Attention all students. This is a protest-free zone. Participation or organization of political activism on campus may result in expulsion or possible incarceration."

The surrounding students boo the announcement. The security guards are becoming anxious and impatient as the students continue to throw garbage in their direction. Some students launch fireworks at them and toss burning bags of dog shit.

Gregory leans close to Elias. "I don't know, man. This is getting out of control. I think we should go back to the dorms."

The lead security guard pulls out a megaphone and speaks to the crowd. He says, "This assembly is against school policy. Everyone must disperse at once. Go back to your dorms. Return to class. This is your only warning."

Jake pulls a can of beer from his eighteen-pack and grips it like a baseball.

The lead security guard continues, "If you fail to follow our orders we are permitted to use force. Those who remain will be expelled from the university and faced with fines or jail time. If you value your education, you will disperse immediately."

Some students separate from the crowd and head back to their classes, but many remain. Jake throws his unopened beer as hard as he can at the crowd of security guards and pegs the leader directly in the helmet so hard that he stumbles back and drops his megaphone.

The lead security guard regains his composure and lifts his shield. He turns to his coworkers.

He yells, "That's it. Let's go."

The row of armored security guards charges forward. They attack the students, slamming them with their shields and hitting them with batons. Several students engage the security guards, jumping at them to push back their shields or throw burning trash at them. Tear gas is shot into the crowd. Only a small minority of the students run away from the threat.

Gregory grabs Elias by the arm. "We have to go."

But Elias charges into the crowd, heading for Roe. Both Jake and Roe are holding their ground, throwing beers at the security guards and yelling profanities at them. Elias rushes to Roe's side, getting between her and the guards waving their batons around.

"Fuck off, pigs!" she yells.

Elias grabs Roe by the arm, trying to pull her back. But she doesn't let up. She's ready to fight. Gregory comes in and helps Elias, but they can't get Roe to leave. She kicks at the riot shields and flips off the men in black armor.

Jake bursts through a shield and grapples with one of the security guards. He is pushed to the ground and the guard puts a knee in his back. Jake cries out, struggling to get out of his grip.

Roe runs up to the security guard holding Jake and kicks him in the helmet.

"Racists!" she screams.

It isn't enough to get Jake free, but it draws another security guard's attention to Roe. Elias and Gregory run to Roe and grab her. Elias gets between Roe and the security guard, trying to hold her back.

"We need to get out of here," he says.

"Fuck that!" Roe screams.

As Elias pushes on Roe and Gregory pulls her from behind, the security guard comes in and swings his baton. Time slows down. The baton misses Elias and pegs Roe in the side of the head. Spit flies out of her mouth as she falls back. Before she hits the ground, she loses consciousness and everyone around her explodes into clouds of smoke and disappears down her throat.

Elias finds himself in a new world with swirling clouds and a red sky. Everything is much dimmer than it was before. It's like a tornado is about to hit down. Gregory is with him, and so is the security guard who hit Roe, Jake, and the guard pinning him to the ground, as well as three other protestors.

Elias helps Roe to her feet. "Are you okay?"

Roe's eyes turn black. Goat horns grow from her head. Her skin turns to porcelain.

"Yeah, I feel good," she says. A smile curls on her face. "I feel like killing some pigs."

She pulls out a knife and stabs the security guard who hit her with his baton. She pushes the blade under his helmet and drives it into his throat. The large man clutches at his neck and falls over.

She looks at Elias, licking the bloody knife. "This is fun. Isn't it, Eliot?"

Then she runs away, into the crowd, cutting everyone she comes across. Elias steps back and gets a good look at his situation. The protestors are now cardboard cutout people holding signs and chanting nonsensical words.

The security guards surrounding them are monstrous pig mutant people ten feet tall.

The three protestors look around, confused about where they are. Gregory grabs Elias' arm and pulls him close.

He cries, "Holy shit, we're here, aren't we? We're in Roe's dreams."

Elias nods. "She got knocked out. We're all in this together."

The security guard pinning Jake to the ground stands up, letting the student free. Jake stands up and the two of them scan the surroundings.

"What happened?" the security guard asks. "Where are we?"

Jake steps away from the armored man and goes toward Elias and Gregory, a look of shock on his face.

"We're fucked," Gregory says. "We're so fucked…"

Jake looks around at the cardboard cutout people and the monstrous pig men in riot gear. "What the fuck is going on?"

"We're in Roe's dream," Elias says.

Gregory adds, "If we die here, we die in real life."

Jake looks at them with a confused face. "What the fuck are you talking about?"

The giant pig men pull out massive cleavers and charge the crowd. They slash through the cardboard cutout people until they get to one of the human protesters. A pig man drives its cleaver through the protester and cuts him in half. The other two protesters scream and run.

Jake, Gregory, and Elias step back.

"We just have to survive until Roe wakes up," Elias says.

"How long will that be?" Jake asks.

"I have no idea."

The cardboard cutout people resist the pig men. They rush at them, shoving the humans in their direction. Elias and Jake try to resist, but they are pushed by the crowd in the direction of the jagged, rusty cleavers. The pig men slash at the crowd, cutting them down like wheat as they snort and growl, their pig faces protruding from their riot gear helmets, snot dripping down their snouts.

Roe leads the mob toward the pig men, screaming and cheering, cutting at them with her knife without fear. When the three men look at her, Gregory shakes his head, staring at her as if she's more terrifying than the monsters in riot gear.

"Stay away from her," Gregory says. "We have to get as far away from her as possible.

Gregory goes into a panic. He forces his way out of the crowd of cardboard people and runs for the dorm alongside one of the protestors. But before he gets far, a new army of pig men appears on all sides of them. They number ten times those at the front of the line. When Gregory sees them, he stops in his tracks and tries to run back. But the pig men charge like an army of barbarians. They cut him down and trample his body, then decapitate the other protestor on their way to engage the mob.

Jake yells, "Gregory!"

Jake tries to run to his friend's body to see if he's still alive, but Elias tugs him back, pulling him by the shirt to get him away from the pig men.

"We have to get deeper in the crowd," Elias says.

Jake looks at him with a terrified face. "What the fuck is this? This can't be real!"

"It *is* real."

Elias looks over at the front line of cardboard protesters. The surviving security guard curls into a ball as the pig men pass him, but they don't attack the cowering man as though he's one of them. The security guard covers his head, crying and whimpering in a panic.

When Elias catches sight of Roe, she is engaging the pig men with her knife, stabbing at their shields.

Elias says, "Come on. We have to help her."

Elias tugs on Jake's arm, but Jake resists.

"I thought she was the cause of all this," Jake says.

"She'll get hurt, too," Elias explains. "It's like what happened with Mikel. If she is hurt or killed in her dreams it will happen in the real world."

"What the hell are you talking about?" Jake asks.

"We have to save her."

Jake pulls himself from his grip. "Dude, she's a lost cause. Let's get out of here."

Elias shakes his head at Jake. "I'm going."

He pushes forward, heading for the front line. He squeezes his way through cardboard people to get to Roe. When he reaches her, he grabs her by the arm and pulls her back just before a cleaver swings at her head. She falls into Elias' arms. When she sees him, she smiles and stares at him with her black ball eyes.

She says, "Eliot, you came to rescue me…"

Elias pulls her to safety and gets her to her feet.

"Are you okay?" he asks.

"Yeah, I'm perfect," she says, her voice becoming deep and demonic. "Now help me kill all these dirty rotten pigs."

She tries to rush off, but he grabs her by the wrist. "No, we have to go back for Jake."

"Blake?" she asks. "He's here, too? I love Blake!"

"Let's go find him," he tells her.

Elias pulls her away from the front lines, taking her back the way he came.

"I want to cut him open and wrap his intestines around my whole body," she says.

As Roe presses her knife lovingly to her cheek, Elias keeps pushing her forward.

"No, you don't," he tells her. "Jake's your friend."

She smiles. "I know. That's why I want to do it."

They keep moving until they see Jake within the crowd of cardboard cutout protestors ahead of them. Before they can reach him, four pig men come in. They surround him with bloody cleavers. Jake falls to the ground, holding up his hands to beg for mercy. But they don't listen to him. They lower their blades into him all at once, then chop maniacally, slashing at him without pity. When Elias and Roe see it happen, Elias stops in his tracks with a look of shock in his eyes. Roe holds out her hand and screams.

She screams, "No! Not Blake! I wanted to gut him myself!"

Then she laughs, admiring his insides being torn from his body.

Elias grabs Roe and pulls her back. "There's nothing we can do."

Roe turns to him and holds him close. Her fingers crawl up his chest and she looks deeply into his eyes.

She says, "But, Eliot... I need to hurt someone. If I don't I'm going to catch fire and burn up."

Flames appear on her clothes, crawling up her back. She points her knife at him, poking the tip of the blade into the flesh beneath his chin.

She asks, "Can I cut you? Just a little bit?"

Elias holds his head back, trembling. He lifts his hands in surrender.

"I'll be gentle," she says.

But before she gets a chance to dig her knife in, the world dissolves around them.

When they are back in the real world, Elias falls to the ground. He sees Roe next to him, her clothes on fire and burning up her back. Elias takes off his jacket and rushes to Roe. He puts out the fire, patting it down as she looks around with confusion on her face.

The security guard who was in the dream world with them is lying on the ground. He looks up at Elias with fear in his eyes and gets himself to his feet. Then he turns tail and runs away, heading for the campus gate. Elias looks back and sees the sole surviving protestor who is in so much shock he can't even move.

The protest is over. The security guards are picking up the remaining protestors and escorting them off campus. Roe pushes Elias' jacket off of her and tries to stand up.

"What happened?" she asks.

She falls back, too weak to get up. Elias lifts her off the ground, cradling her in his arms.

"It's okay," he says. "I'll get you out of here."

Elias carries Roe through the crowd of protestors and security guards. Clouds of tear gas billow around him. Coughing as he breathes it in, he pushes on. Bringing Roe to safety.

Roe looks up at him with a dazed look in her eyes. "Where's Jake?" she asks.

Elias says, "He's gone. They're all gone."

Elias doesn't stop moving until he carries her all the way to Crestridge Dorm. As they get to the steps to the building, Roe's eyes flutter and become weak.

"I'm tired," she says.

"Don't go to sleep. You have a concussion. You have to stay awake."

"But I'm so tired…"

Her eyes drift shut.

Elias tries to keep her awake, but her consciousness fades until her body goes limp in his arms and he fades into a cloud of smoke.

CHAPTER
NINE

The sky changes to swirling red clouds as Elias carries Roe toward the dormitory. When he looks down at her face, he sees her cracked porcelain skin and black tears flowing from her closed eyes. The door to the dorm is broken open, hanging on the hinges. He pushes through them and goes inside. Then he takes her up the stairwell to the fifth floor.

The hallway is even more dilapidated than ever. There's no electricity. The ground is covered in mold and puddles of black fluid. The floor is warped, the wallpaper dripping in long soggy strips. The ceiling is collapsing. Half the building has crumbled and reveals a wide-open sky. Alien vegetation grows from the floor under the red sun. Dark blue grass blows in a light breeze beneath bone-white bushes that produce black roses and spiky purple fruits. It's like a hundred years have passed since the last dream.

Elias carries Roe to their room. He pushes through the raggedy blankets that hang from the ceiling. The room is dim, lit only by the red sky coming in from the window. He lays her down on her bed.

Roe opens her black eyes and peers up at him.

"Eliot?" she asks.

"It's Elias," he says.

"What's going on?" she asks. "Where are we?"

"We're in your dream," he tells her. "You had a concussion and fell asleep again."

"If I fell asleep with a concussion, I'll go into a coma. I might never wake up again."

Elias shakes his head. "That's just a myth. You'll be fine."

Roe lifts her hand to Elias' face and stares deep into his eyes. "You'll stay with me, won't you? Even if I never wake up again?"

"Do I have a choice?" Elias asks.

Roe smiles up at him, her skin cracking around the cheeks. "No, I guess you don't."

He sits down on the bed next to her, watching her carefully, making sure she's okay.

"Why are you so nice to me, Eliot?" she asks. "Most guys only care about me for one thing. You're not like any of them."

Elias shrugs. He pulls away from her and looks at their decrepit dorm room.

"You've always been nice to me," he says. "Even though you never needed to be. You're also an amazing artist. Far better than I am. I always wanted an artist friend like you."

Roe snickers at him. "Nobody's ever called me an amazing artist before."

Elias looks down at her. "Actually, calling your work amazing is almost an understatement. It's better than that. It's phenomenal. I really look up to you. I wish I could have your confidence."

Roe pats him on the leg. "Oh, Eliot. You're such a flatterer. I'm not that good. I only draw for fun."

Elias looks her in the eyes. "No, you're amazing. I've flipped through your portfolio. It's the best art I've ever seen from anyone our age. The whole reason I came to college was to meet someone like you, someone who would inspire me to do better work. I want nothing more than to be your friend."

Roe laughs. "You're so weird."

"I'm not joking," he says. "This school is bullshit. I won't learn anything here. But having a friend like you is worth a thousand teachers. It's worth all the money it costs to come here. I could learn so much from you."

She can't keep a straight face. She shoves her horns into her pillow and giggles at his words. Then she grips his thighs with her claw-like fingers and giggles with enthusiasm.

"I really like you, Eliot," she says. "You're such a freak."

Elias looks away. He places his hand over the claws on his thigh, keeping them from cutting in any deeper.

"I like you, too," he says.

There is silence between them for a while. They sit on the bed together, staring into the dimly lit room, breathing in the musty air.

After several hours, Roe says, "I don't think I'm going to wake up. I think we're stuck here."

Elias looks at her. "You'll wake up eventually. You have to."

Roe shakes her head. "It's been too long. If I haven't woken up yet I don't think I ever will."

Elias looks down at his hands, but doesn't say anything.

Roe sits up and pulls his face toward hers, to get him to pay closer attention.

"If you are trapped here with me, will you be okay with that? Will you live in my dreams with me?"

Elias pulls away from her. "I don't know."

"Why not?" she cries.

He inches away. "You always try to kill me whenever you're dreaming. I can't trust you."

Roe shakes her head. "I don't feel like killing you anymore. I just don't want to be alone."

Elias looks at her. "You've killed a lot of people. Gregory told me all about the men who disappeared before I came to this school."

Roe smiles. "Who cares about them? They weren't you."

"What's the difference between me and them?" Elias asks.

"They didn't interest me like you do."

"So you don't regret killing them?"

A smile curls on Roe's lips. "I had so much fun killing them. I would kill them a thousand times over. I wish I could kill them again. If only I could…"

As Elias pulls back at her words, she grabs onto him and draws him closer.

"But I won't kill you," she says. "You're my friend."

"And they weren't your friends?" Elias asks.

She shrugs at him. "Maybe they were a little while I was awake. But they meant nothing to me in the sleeping world. It was too much fun to kill them. I couldn't resist."

Elias looks at her. "But you won't kill me?"

She smiles. "How could I kill my Eliot? I'm far too in love with you."

"You barely know me," he says.

"I know you enough," she says. "I know that if we're trapped in this dream together for the rest of my life that I'll never be bored. I'll never be lonely. I might hurt you from time to time, but I'll never do it out of hate."

Elias looks away, feeling uncomfortable by her side. He is about to stand up and walk away when Roe grabs him and pulls him close to her chest.

"Don't go," she says. "I'll be better. I'm not really a bad person."

Elias sighs and says, "You have to promise you won't hurt me."

"I promise I won't. I'll be whatever you want me to be."

"I just want you to be you, the person you are when you're awake."

Roe shakes her head. "That's not the real me."

"Neither is the you in your dreams," Elias says.

Roe looks down at her hands, pulling herself away from him.

"Maybe I am," she says.

Then she looks up at him. "But you'll stay with me anyway, won't you? You know, if I never wake up?"

"Do I have a choice?" he asks.

"You always have a choice," she says.

He thinks about it for a moment, then lets out a sigh.

He looks at her and says, "Then I guess I choose to stay with you."

Roe smiles and hugs him close to her.

As he feels her cracked porcelain skin against his cheek, her horns pressed against his skull, he wonders why he said such a thing. He doesn't want anything to do with this woman, not the version of Roe that lives in her dreams. He just wants to be a normal student in a normal school. He just wants to be an artist. He doesn't want to be trapped in a dream world with a psychotic freak with blood lust. He doesn't want to be killed like all of her other roommates and boyfriends.

But when Roe curls herself around him, her heart beating against his chest, he wonders if he couldn't stay like this for longer. He wonders if he couldn't just give up everything and stay in her arms forever.

Elias and Roe stay in the dream world for what seems like a hundred years. They spend most of their time painting pictures together. Roe can materialize all of the paint and canvases that they need. They teach each other how to be better artists. Roe shows Elias how to paint without being such a perfectionist and he encourages her how to take her art more seriously. In time, they both become great artists, far better than they were in the waking world. The paintings that Elias creates are so breathtaking that he wishes he could display them in a gallery in the real world. He wishes he could show more people his work than just Roe in her dreams.

Although she used to look like a horrific demon to Elias, he has gotten used to the appearance of this Roe. He's even forgotten what she used to look like when she was awake. But over time, her appearance changes. Her porcelain skin stops crumbling. It becomes smooth and delicate, like that of a new doll. Her horns recede into her head. Her eyes go from black to glowing bright purple. She still looks far from human, but is now inhuman in a beautiful way rather than a horrific one.

With Elias' help, Roe learns how to control her dreams. She discovers how to reshape their world into anything she wants. Instead of a decaying, broken building in a horrific landscape, she transforms Crestridge Dorm into a luxurious resort next to a vast ocean of pink waves crashing against blue sand beaches.

It becomes like heaven for them, living in a fantasy world of Roe's creation, just the two of them. They have elegant meals on the beach of barbequed alien meats and fancy colorful cocktails that smoke and bubble. They don't need to eat to survive and alcohol doesn't quite get them drunk, but it is enjoyable enough to indulge on occasion. All of the flavors are strange and difficult to compare to any food from the real world, but Elias gets used to it and grows to like Roe's meals, even though each dish tastes completely different every single time they eat it.

Whenever they're bored, Roe brings them to a new place and makes them a new home. They go from a fairy tale cottage in a magical forest to a penthouse apartment in a futuristic city to a space station in orbit around an alien planet more majestic than Jupiter or Saturn. Anything Roe can imagine becomes their new world. And every single moment in the dream is the best moment of Elias' life.

In time, they fall deeply in love with each other. Roe insists they get married at the top of a giant tree that's big enough to hold an entire planet, filled with fairies and elves that come to the ceremony as wedding guests. It is more magical than any wedding that ever could have been possible in the real world. They dance to fairy violin music while floating in the sky among the rainbows and butterflies and falling pink leaves from the world tree.

It isn't long before Roe becomes pregnant. They are filled with the fear and excitement of becoming new parents, creating the perfect world where they can raise their child—an old wooden mansion among a field of sunflowers that stretches as far as the eyes can see. They aren't sure what it will be like to raise a child in a dream world, without any friends or teachers or any real people besides the two of them, but they know their offspring will have a childhood full of magic and wonder, one that any child on Earth could only dream of having.

Roe is nine months pregnant, lying in the middle of a heart-shaped bed the size of a small bedroom with fluffy pink sheets and massive pillows designed for a princess. Elias lies next to her, staring at her swollen porcelain belly with flowers painted onto the sides like tattoos. She taps on the porcelain with her long violet fingernails, like she's trying to communicate with her fetus, hoping that it will knock back.

"Have you decided on a name?" Elias asks.

They have been trying to agree on one for months, but Roe is too indecisive. She changes her mind every other week.

"I think I know this time," she says. "If it's a boy I want to call him Xavier."

"Xavier? Like Professor X?"

"Who's Professor X?"

"You know, from the X-Men. The bald guy in the wheelchair."

Roe shakes her head. "Never heard of him."

Elias nods. He sometimes forgets that she doesn't have the same memories of the real world as he does. Since she's the subconscious version of Roe, she doesn't have the same understanding of the world as the one that lives in reality.

"I like Xavier," she says. "It sounds like the name of a noble knight from a magical kingdom. That is the kind of son I think we should have, one who goes on adventures that I can create for him."

Elias smiles and agrees with her.

Then he asks, "And what if it's a girl?"

"It's between Eve and Eilowny. Eve because I will give her a world like the garden of Eden. Eilowny because it sounds like the name of a fairy. If I have a daughter I want her to be a fairy. I'll even give her fairy wings."

Elias laughs. "Of course she should have fairy wings."

"Whatever the name, I want our child to have the most magical childhood anyone could ever dream of."

Elias agrees. "Any name will be fine. I'm sure it will be the most beautiful baby in the world as long as it's yours."

Roe smiles and looks over at him with her big purple eyes and takes his hand in hers. She places it on her warm porcelain stomach and stares him in the eyes.

"Are you happy you decided to stay with me?" she asks him. "Even though you didn't have a choice."

Elias nods. "I'd rather be here than anywhere else in the world."

"You mean that?"

Tears pool up in her purple eyes.

"Of course I do."

He leans in and kisses her on the cheek. Before he pulls away, she grabs him by the back of the neck and shoves his lips into hers. She kisses him with all of the passion in her being.

As she releases his lips and presses her hard porcelain forehead against his, she says, "I'll always be with you. I'll always make you as happy as you are now."

He smiles at her. "I couldn't want anything more."

But as she tries to kiss him again, his face begins to disappear. His lips fall through hers as he turns into a smoke-like substance. He backs away and looks at his fading hands.

"What's going on?" he asks, looking into her eyes with panic.

She sits up and tries to grab him, but she can't get hold of him.

"I'm waking up," Roe says. "The dream is ending."

Elias shakes his head. "That's impossible. I thought you were in a coma."

Roe shakes her head, her tears of joy turning to tears of horror. "You can't go. You have to stay with me forever."

"I don't want to go," he says, his eyes tearing up as much as hers.

As his body dissipates more and more, Roe cries, "Don't let it end like this. I never want this dream to end."

"Neither do I…"

A look of desperation on Roe's face as the world begins to fade around them.

"Promise me you'll come back to me," she tells him.

"I promise," he says. "I'll do whatever I can."

Then they try to kiss one more time, despite not being able to touch one another, just trying to be as close to one another as they can before their heavenly world comes to an end.

CHAPTER
TEN

When Elias awakes in the real world, his tears are still rolling down his cheeks. His lips are still pursed. His arms are still out as though embracing somebody who isn't there.

He opens his eyes to find himself standing in the middle of a hospital room. Roe is on a bed, hooked up to machines. It appears as though she was in a coma for a very long time. As she comes to, she moans out in pain. Her body is stiff and sluggish, barely able to sit up straight. She's lost a ton of weight, her arms and face just skin and bones. Elias can't believe the sight of her.

When she regains her senses, Roe looks around the room in a panic.

"What the fuck?" she cries. "Where the hell am I?"

She doesn't seem to notice Elias yet. He goes to her and asks, "Are you okay?"

When she sees him standing there, she says, "Elias? What happened? Why am I in a hospital?"

Elias goes to her side. "You got hurt during the protest and were put into a coma."

She wheezes at the pain as she tries to move. "What the fuck…"

Elias grabs her by the hand. It is bony and fragile. Her fingers feel almost grown together, like she doesn't have the strength to separate them.

"Do you remember anything?" he asks her. His voice is nervous and desperate. He has to know if she remembers anything from the long dream he's been living in with her.

She shakes her head. "I just remember fighting with the campus security after things got out of control."

"No, not the protest," Elias says. "Do you remember anything that happened after that?"

She looks at him with a confused face. "Like what?"

"I mean after you fell asleep. Do you remember your dream?"

"Dream?" Her face becomes annoyed. "No. Why would I give a fuck about my dream?"

Elias becomes frantic. He squeezes her hand tighter. "You don't remember us being together in your dream?"

She becomes frightened of him. "What the fuck are you talking about?"

Elias can't believe what he's saying, but he's unable to control himself. "You have to remember. We were together there for so long. We got married. We were going to have a child together. You have to remember."

She pushes him back with what little strength she has. "What's wrong with you? Why are you acting so weird?"

"You have to go back to sleep," he says. "You made me promise to come back to you. I have to see you again, the version of you in your dreams."

She backs up, holding her hands up, terrified of him.

"Are you fucking insane?" she cries.

He keeps his distance, but won't let it go. "I'm not lying. I promise this really happened. When you sleep, you bring people into your dreams. I've been living there with you since you've been in your coma."

As Elias inches closer, she freaks out. "Get away from me! You're sick in the head!"

Elias doesn't know what else to do but cry. He bursts into tears, ready to collapse on the floor. "But we were going to have a baby together. We made a life for each other in your dreams. It was so perfect. Everything was perfect."

As Elias says this, Roe ignores his words. She is too busy focusing on a lump below her covers.

"What the…" she says in a panic.

When she pulls the blanket down, she notices her swollen belly for the first time. She rips open her hospital gown and feels her stomach to make sure that it's real. It seems impossible to her, but it's true. She's nine months pregnant.

Although Roe has no idea what has happened, Elias knows that it's his child. He's sure that when she got pregnant in her dream that she also got pregnant in real life. It's their baby, the same one they were going to raise in the dream world.

When she sees her pregnant belly, Roe just screams at the top of her lungs. There's nothing else she can do.

Elias tries to calm her down, but doesn't know what to say. Instead, he uses it as proof to back up his story.

"See, I told you," he says. "That's our baby. You got pregnant in your dream. You have to believe me."

Before he can say any more, a nurse bursts into the room, rushing to the sound of Roe's screams. She locks eyes on Elias, shocked to see him standing there.

"How did you get in here?" the nurse cries.

Elias doesn't know how to answer that. He opens his mouth to speak, but Roe interrupts him.

"Get him away from me," she cries, pointing at Elias. "Get him the fuck out of here!"

The nurse steps between Elias and Roe and pushes him toward the door.

"Okay, you need to go," the nurse says.

"But I have to talk to her…" Elias says.

The nurse shoves him out of the door, blocking the doorway so that he can't get inside.

She yells to another nurse in the hallway, "Get security."

Before she can push him all the way out, Elias calls out to Roe. "It's the truth. You have to believe me!"

Just before the nurse closes the door in his face, he yells, "I'm sorry."

But he doesn't think Roe could hear him. He listens through the door to the nurse trying to calm Roe down as two security staff members charge down the hallway toward him. He doesn't fight. He lets them escort him away from the hospital room, wiping tears from his eyes, feeling like his whole world has fallen apart in front of him.

A couple of hours later, Elias' mother arrives at the hospital. She meets him in the waiting room where he's been told to stay put, kept under watch by a lone security guard blocking his path from the rest of the hospital.

When she sees him, his mother's eyes are full of relief and happiness. She hugs him close without saying a word. Elias barely recognizes his mother. He doesn't know how long he's been in the dream world, but his mother seems to have aged quite a bit since the last time he's seen her. She must have been torn apart from stress and worry.

"Where were you all this time?" she asks, as she pulls away from his hug. "I thought you were dead."

He shakes his head. "I've been fine."

Her voice is shaking and barely able to get her words out between sobs. "I thought you were dead. So many students went missing at your school at the same time as you. Nobody knew what happened to any of them."

She looks at him waiting for an answer, but he doesn't know what to say. He just shakes his head and tells her, "I don't know how to explain it. You wouldn't believe me if I told you."

She pries further, "Were you abducted? Were you safe?"

"I wasn't in danger. I was happy."

"Why didn't you call?"

"I couldn't…"

"What do you mean you couldn't?"

"It's hard to explain. I got married."

Her eyes light up. "What do you mean you got married?"

He shakes his head, not wanting to explain further. He just hugs her again and says, "I'm sorry I put you through so much."

She hugs him back with as much strength as she can muster and says, "You can tell me later. I'm just happy you're alive."

"It's good to see you, too," he says.

In his mother's embrace, he realizes how glad he is to see his mother again. If he had stayed in the dream world forever, he never would have seen her ever again. Although he wishes he could go back, he's dying to return no matter the consequences, he's still happy to be with her. She's his only family member, the only person who's ever been there for him throughout his entire life. He can't believe that he was once okay with living the rest of his life without ever seeing her again.

When she pulls away, she says, "Let's go home. You can tell me where you were in your own time."

But before she can lead him toward the exit, Elias resists.

He says, "I can't. I have to wait for the police."

"The police?" she asks, a look of worry spreading on her face.

"They want to ask me some questions," he says. "Hopefully it won't take long."

As he says this, two police officers walk through the entrance to the hospital. A security guard leads them toward Elias and his mother.

"Elias Thompson?" a police officer asks him.

"Yeah?" Elias asks.

The policeman pulls out a pair of handcuffs. "We'd like you to come with us."

When they go to him, Elias doesn't resist, but his mother goes into a panic.

"What is this all about?" she cries. "What did he do?"

The policeman tells her, "He's been accused of sexual assault."

He says this in such a stern tone, without concern for how it would affect a mother whose child has been accused of such a thing.

"That's impossible," she tells them. "He would never do such a thing. I raised him to treat women with respect."

The cop doesn't look her in the eyes as they put her son in handcuffs. "Please don't interfere, ma'am."

But Elias' mother won't let it go. She follows them out of the hospital toward their car parked out front.

"I don't understand," she yells. "Elias, what happened? Tell me it's not true."

Elias is unable to look his mother in the eyes as he explains himself. "It wasn't assault. She just doesn't remember anything."

As the policemen guide Elias into the back of the cop car, she says, "What's that supposed to mean?"

But he doesn't have time to explain. The cops close the door and get into the car. They drive away without saying another word.

Elias looks back at his mother standing alone in the street with a look of horror on her face, covering her mouth with her hand. The moment she finally thought she got her son back, he was taken away from her again.

The DNA test comes back proving that Elias is the father of Roe's child. Everyone is confused about how it happened. At first, they thought he raped her in her sleep while they were roommates in college, but that was impossible because the time of conception was several months into her coma. They thought that he must have broken into the hospital and raped her there, but the hospital staff claimed that it was impossible. There was no way somebody could have done that. The security footage in the hospital didn't show anyone matching Elias' description, nobody suspicious had ever broken into Roe's room. There was no reasonable explanation for the pregnancy. No possible way it could have happened. But the DNA evidence is all the proof the courts needed to convict him.

Elias is sentenced to ten years in prison. His lawyers tell him that he should be happy that he got off so easy. If they had better proof, the prosecutors would have given him the maximum sentence possible. It was the rarest case that the courts had ever seen.

It takes a couple of years for Elias to become accustomed to life in prison. The experience is both better and worse than what he expected based on how prison is portrayed in movies. Violence and sexual abuse are not as common as he expected they would be. He prepared himself for that. He even had plans to kick someone's ass on his first day and make friends with the toughest people he could find, but none of that was necessary. The only abuse he got was from fathers of young women who found out he was a sexual predator and wanted to kick his ass out of revenge, like they were standing up for Roe even though they never met her before. But they never did anything but threaten him. He never got his ass kicked even though he feared he would daily.

The worst part of prison is the tension. Elias spends every day on edge, worried about what will happen to him. He's never experienced stress like this, not even when his life was in danger in Roe's dreams. But eventually, he gets used to it. He spends his days focused on his art. His mother sends him supplies and he's able to paint and draw to his heart's content. He's become an amazing artist because of his time in Roe's dream world. He took all of his experience with him into the real world. He has made some friends in prison because of his artwork and has started designing tattoos for some of the inmates and even a book cover for one of them who has become a self-published author during his incarceration.

But even though his skills have become so great, Elias doesn't think he has much of a chance of becoming a professional artist once he gets out of jail. He knows that his reputation is tarnished. No gallery will ever want to display the art of a sexual predator. No legitimate publisher will allow his artwork on book covers. No company will hire him for graphic design. While he's in jail, people might fight for his right to be treated well during his incarceration. But once he's free, those same people will fight to keep him out of employment. Nobody wants a person with his past to succeed in the outside world. He doesn't know if he disagrees with them. He wouldn't buy the art of a sexual predator either. But if he can't do art for a living, he doesn't know what else to do with his life. He plans to still create artwork for as long as he can, no matter what happens. He doesn't have anything else going for him. He just has the worlds that he creates with the paint on his brush.

Every day that passes, he still has memories of the time he spent in Roe's dreams. He still longs for those times. He feels guilty that he wishes Roe never woke up from her coma, wishing he could have spent eternity with her. He knows it's selfish, but he can't help but feel this way. Roe and her subconscious self were two different people and the one he fell in love with doesn't exist in this world. He wishes it was different. He wishes the one in the real world fell in love with him. He wishes that he could have had a life with her, with their child. He would have wanted them to be great artists together. They could have done anything with their lives.

But even if this fantasy became true, he would have had to deal with the Roe in her dreams. He wonders if it was possible to be with both of them, to love them equally in the waking world as well as in her dreams. He would have had two different relationships with two amazing women who were both named Roe. But he knows that it's impossible. He could never have had it both ways. If he knew Roe was going to wake up one day, he never would have decided to have a baby with her subconscious self. If only he held back everything would have been different. His life wouldn't have been over before it started.

Eight years into his incarceration, Elias gets a visitor he wasn't expecting. His mother comes to see him four times a year like clockwork, around Thanksgiving, Christmas, Easter, and his birthday, but it's months away from her next visit. He's surprised that Roe is the one who wants to see him. After everything that happened, he was sure that she'd never want to see him again.

He's brought out to the visitation room and sees her sitting there with an eight-year-old girl. He recognizes Roe right away, even though she's aged quite a bit. Despite still being in her twenties, she looks well into her thirties, aged from being a single mom for so many years.

She doesn't appear excited to see him, a look of anxiety and annoyance on her face. But the girl by his side has the opposite expression. The child is lit up with amazement, smiling and waving at him. It's as though she knows exactly what her father looks like, even though they've never met before. Elias can see himself in her. He never knew what his daughter looked like, but upon first glance, she's everything he imagined she would be. She's the most beautiful little girl he ever laid eyes on.

When he sits down, he finds himself shaking with anticipation. He never thought he'd see Roe again. He can't believe she's right there in front of him.

"I'm surprised you're here," Elias says.

Roe doesn't show any emotion as she sits across from him.

"Your daughter wanted to meet you," Roe says. "I thought it was a bad idea but she insisted."

When Roe looks at her daughter, the little girl leans in closer and tells her mother, "He looks just like him. Only older."

Roe doesn't respond to her daughter. She keeps her eyes locked on Elias. "Her name's Eilowny."

When she says this, Elias' eyes light up. "Like in the dream?"

Roe's face is confused.

He explains, "That's what you wanted to call her in your dream. Either that or Eve."

Roe shakes her head. "How did you know about that? After she was born, those two names came into my head. I chose Eilowny because it sounded like—"

"The name of a fairy!" Elias cries.

When he says this, Roe's face becomes flustered. She looks away.

"I'm sorry, I have to go," Roe says.

She gets up, ready to leave the room. Elias realizes he shouldn't have said anything about the dream world. He knows he must have traumatized her back when she woke up from the coma when he told her about their life together in her dreams, probably thinking he was a psychotic freak. He doesn't blame her for wanting to run away.

"I'm sorry," Elias says. "Did I say something wrong?"

"I need some air," she tells him.

But when she walks away, she doesn't take her daughter with her. She leaves the little girl with him, as though she is only leaving the room temporarily and plans to return for her daughter at a later time.

As Elias sits there across from his daughter, he doesn't know what to say. He just stares at her, wondering what her life has been like all this time. He hopes that she's happy. He hopes that Roe has been giving her a good childhood despite raising her under such horrific circumstances.

But as they sit there for a moment, it's Eilowny who breaks the silence first.

The girl says, "She told me to tell you that she misses you."

When Elias hears this, he doesn't understand who she's talking about.

He asks, "Who? Your mother?"

"Not the outside one," Eilowny says. "My dream mommy. She told me to tell you that she still loves you, that she wishes you were still with her."

When Elias hears this, his hands begin to shake. He can't believe what she's telling him.

133

"You've been to your mother's dreams?" he asks.

The girl smiles up at him and nods her head.

"I see my dream mommy almost every night," Eilowny says. "She's so nice. She lets me fly with the fairies and ride unicorns on top of rainbows. She made me a castle filled with toys and every night is my birthday. And she never yells at me. Not ever. I wish she was my real mommy."

Elias can't help but smile. He never thought about it before, but of course, Roe's daughter would be taken into her dreams. Of course, the subconscious version of Roe would meet her and be with her as mother and daughter. It's probably been going on for all of Eilowny's life, ever since she was born. He wishes he was there with them to experience it all.

"She *is* your real mom," Elias tells her. "She's the one who conceived you. If Roe never woke up from her coma you would have been born in that world and lived there for your entire life."

When he says this, Eilowny's eyes light up with excitement. A smile grows wide on her face.

"That's what she said!" the girl cries. "She said I was supposed to grow up with her. I wish I could stay in the dream world always. All the kids at school think I'm weird and crazy whenever I talk about it. They make fun of me all the time. I hate my life outside of my mom's dreams."

She pouts and puts her elbows on the table, resting her hands on her chubby cheeks. Elias can't help but smile at how cute she is.

"I know what you mean," Elias says. "I hate my life outside of your mother's dreams as well. I wish more than anything that I could have been there with you two this whole time. I would give anything to be."

His words brighten the little girl's eyes. She sits up straight, happy to have found the only other person in the world who understands the paradise that she goes to whenever her mother is asleep.

"Then why don't you?" the girl asks. "My dream mommy says that we can be together as a family if only my real mom goes into a coma again. If you hit her really hard in the head then maybe she'll go to sleep forever. You should do it once she comes back."

When Elias hears her words, the smile falls from his face. He realizes just how messed up his daughter has become. Living in two worlds with two different mothers has psychologically damaged her. Although he wishes he could return to the dream world, he would never do something so horrible.

Elias shakes his head. "Don't say that. It's not funny."

Eilowny becomes quiet, surprised by his words. "But my dream mommy said that you'd want to…"

Elias speaks with a stern voice. "I would never do something so horrible. Not only would it never work, but it's not fair to your real mother. She loves you too much."

Eilowny shakes her head. "No she doesn't. She's always mean to me. She's at work all day and when she comes home she yells at me. I hate her."

Elias shakes his head. "You don't hate her."

"I do, too!"

"She only works that much so that she can take care

of you. My mother did the same thing for me."

Eilowny begins to cry. "She said you would do it. She said you would do anything to come back to the dream world."

Elias takes a deep breath. He doesn't know what to say. After thinking it over for a moment, he tells her, "I do want to be with your dream mommy again. But I don't want your real mom to go into a coma. I don't want to hurt her. It wouldn't work anyway. The fact that she went into a coma in the first place was a fluke. It wouldn't happen again."

His words only upset the girl more. Tears fall from her eyes.

"You should be happy with what you have," Elias says, trying to cheer her up. "You have two mothers who love you very much. Being able to go between both worlds is amazing. You can live your life in the real world and still return to the dream world and ride unicorns and do whatever you want. Who cares about what the kids at your school say? They only wish they can do what you can. You have it better than anyone else in the whole world."

As he says this, his daughter's expression brightens a bit.

Elias continues, "You're special, Eilowny. You're the most special girl in the whole world. You should be happy being exactly who you are."

The girl's smile reappears on her face. She wipes the tears from her eyes.

"But what about you?" she asks. "My dream mommy

is so sad without you. She told me that I have to bring you back."

Elias smiles. He's happy that she's so concerned about his relationship with the woman in her mother's dreams.

"Don't worry about me," he says. "I just want *you* to be happy."

The girl looks up at him. She doesn't say it in words, but her eyes tell him, "I'd be happier if you could come with me to the dreams. I have no one to share them with. And my dream mommy is so lonely without you."

He's not sure that's what she's actually wanting to communicate, but Elias imagines it to be true. And the thought of her having those desires make him happier than he's been in a very long time.

Roe takes her daughter to visit him many times over the next couple of years. Eilowny brings him messages from the woman he loves and he sends messages back with her. It's like he's able to correspond with his love while he's incarcerated. He's able to continue his connection to her in a way he never thought possible. And on top of that, he gets to see his daughter grow up before his eyes and they become closer as father and daughter. He counts every day between her visits and makes sure he's as happy and upbeat as he possibly can whenever she's around him. He writes poems for his love that his daughter is excited to memorize and recite to her dream mommy.

It takes time, but eventually Roe comes to understand that Elias and her daughter are speaking the truth. There's just no other explanation for it. She comes to understand that people are capable of entering her subconscious whenever she goes to sleep. But even though she believes it to be true, she's still bothered by it all. She doesn't like the idea that another version of herself has such a close relationship with her daughter. She doesn't like that this woman is in love with her old college roommate whom she once believed raped her while she was in a coma. And on top of that, she now understands what happened to all of the people that went missing when she was younger, from her boyfriends to her roommates to all of her past foster parents. She has to live with the fact that she's responsible for their deaths.

It makes Roe terrified of this person inside of her. She doesn't know if she can trust her with her daughter, even though it is just an unconscious version of herself. She says that she's trying to be as happy and positive as she can so that her subconscious self doesn't take it out on her daughter. Therapy has been helping, but she tells Elias that it's a fear that she's having difficulty getting over.

When Elias' sentence has been served and he's released from prison, Roe asks him to move in with them. At first, he isn't sure if that's such a good idea but he eventually gives in. She lets him stay in a room in her basement, but rarely lets him step foot inside the rest of the house. She knows how much he means to her daughter. And once he gets a job, he's able to help her with the bills and the large debt she stacked up from attending university.

After some time, Roe eventually agrees to let Elias return to her dream world. She doesn't do it for his sake, however, or for the sake of her subconscious self. She does it because she wants somebody to watch out for her daughter while she's inside her dreams. She doesn't particularly like Elias anymore, but she knows him enough to trust that he won't let anything happen to their daughter. It gives her a little peace of mind, even though she's not happy with the situation at all.

Roe tells Elias that she hasn't had luck with any relationships in the past. It turns out that any man she falls for always breaks up with her soon after they start sleeping together. She believes that the version of herself in her dreams doesn't approve of them and always scares them away. None of them have been killed, but they always wake up terrified of Roe and never want to see her again. Roe gave up on the idea of ever being with anyone long ago. Although she hasn't said it, she seems to resent Elias because of this. It's like she thinks it's his fault for letting her inner self fall in love with him.

When it's time to finally go into the dream world, Elias is itching with anticipation. Roe takes a sleeping pill while they are watching a movie in the living room. Eilowny is there with them, complaining to her mom for taking so long to fall asleep. But it only takes half of the movie before she fades out. Elias and Eilowny turn to smoke as Roe falls into unconsciousness. They look at each other, smiling with excitement. Then they disappear down Roe's throat, laughing with more happiness than either of them has felt in a very long time.

They materialize in the same house that Elias remembers from the last day he spent in the dream world. Eilowny is by his side, looking up at him with a delighted expression on her face. He smiles down at her. She takes him by the hand and leads him down the path toward the house, stepping through the field of sunflowers.

"She's going to be so happy to see you," Eilowny tells him.

He squeezes her hand. "Not as happy as I am to see her."

When he sees her standing in the doorway of the house, Elias' heart nearly stops. She's more beautiful than he remembers. Her porcelain skin reflects the bright sunlight, her long dark hair blows in the spring wind, and her bright purple eyes lock onto his in such a loving way. Elias couldn't be any happier than he is at this moment.

He lets go of Eilowny's hand and runs to the woman in the doorway and kisses her with all of his love, holding her tighter than anyone he's held before.

"I've missed you so much," he tells her.

She presses herself against him and rubs her hard hand against his cheek. "It feels like an eternity."

Once Eilowny arrives, they take her by the hand and bring her into their embrace.

"We're finally together," the dream Roe says to them. "After all this time, we're finally a family again."

She takes them by her hands and leads them into their new home. Eilowny runs up the stairs to her room,

140

wanting to show her father all of the toys she's never been able to show anyone before. But before he follows her, Roe grabs him again and pulls him close.

"Just give us a minute," she says to her daughter.

Eilowny looks back and smiles at them from the top of the stairs.

"Don't take long," she tells her dream mother. "I'll be in my room."

When they are alone, Roe turns back to Elias and kisses him again. She wraps her arms around him and presses him to her body, giving him all the love she hasn't been able to give him in the past ten years. Elias can't believe he's really with her. He can't help but cry against her shoulder.

Back when they were in college, this version of Roe has always tried to kill him in her dreams. But after all this time, after all Elias has been through, he now understands that nothing kills him more than the feeling of her in his arms once again.

BONUS SECTION

This is the part of the book where we would have published an afterword by the author but he insisted on drawing a comic strip instead for reasons we don't quite understand.

Thank you for reading my new book, *You Always Try to Kill Me in Your Dreams*. Wasn't it dreamy?

It's me CM3!

So the ending of this book kind of bugs me.

I'm not sure if it's a happy ending, a tragic ending, or a fucked up ending. Maybe it's all of the above.

It seems like a happy ending for Eilowny, a bittersweet ending for Elias, and a tragic ending for Roe.

But what bugs me the most about the ending of the story is imagining what happens next.

Though there is a chance that Roe and Elias will end up being romantically involved at some point.

Because the subconscious version of Roe will not allow her to get into a relationship with any man but Elias, Roe really doesn't have any other romantic options.

She can either be with Elias or stay single. So she might be willing to give it a try, especially when he is the father of her child.

But if that were actually to happen, wouldn't there be jealousy between Roe and her subconscious self?

They might not like sharing Elias, even though they are technically the same person.

It makes me wonder if there's jealous involved when somebody dates a person with dissociative identity disorder.

ABOUT THE AUTHOR

Carlton Mellick III is one of the leading authors of the bizarro fiction subgenre. Since 2001, his books have drawn an international cult following, despite the fact that they have been shunned by most libraries and chain bookstores.

He won the Wonderland Book Award for his novel, *Warrior Wolf Women of the Wasteland*, in 2009. His short fiction has appeared in *Vice Magazine, The Year's Best Fantasy and Horror #16, The Magazine of Bizarro Fiction,* and *Zombies: Encounters with the Hungry Dead*, among others. He is also a graduate of Clarion West, where he studied under the likes of Chuck Palahniuk, Connie Willis, and Cory Doctorow.

He lives in Portland, OR, the bizarro fiction mecca.

Visit him online at **www.carltonmellick.com**

QUICKSAND HOUSE

Tick and Polly have never met their parents before. They live in the same house with them, they dream about them every night, they share the same flesh and blood, yet for some reason their parents have never found the time to visit them even once since they were born. Living in a dark corner of their parents' vast crumbling mansion, the children long for the day when they will finally be held in their mother's loving arms for the first time... But that day seems to never come. They worry their parents have long since forgotten about them.

When the machines that provide them with food and water stop functioning, the children are forced to venture out of the nursery to find their parents on their own. But the rest of the house is much larger and stranger than they ever could have imagined. The maze-like hallways are dark and seem to go on forever, deranged creatures lurk in every shadow, and the bodies of long-dead children litter the abandoned storerooms. Every minute out of the nursery is a constant battle for survival. And the deeper into the house they go, the more they must unravel the mysteries surrounding their past and the world they've grown up in, if they ever hope to meet the parents they've always longed to see.

Like a survival horror rendition of *Flowers in the Attic*, Carlton Mellick III's *Quicksand House* is his most gripping and sincere work to date.

HUNGRY BUG

In a world where magic exists, spell-casting has become a serious addiction. It ruins lives, tears families apart, and eats away at the fabric of society. Those who cast too much are taken from our world, never to be heard from again. They are sent to a realm known as Hell's Bottom—a sorcerer ghetto where everyday life is a harsh struggle for survival. Porcelain dolls crawl through the alleys like rats, arcane scientists abduct people from the streets to use in their ungodly experiments, and everyone lives in fear of the aristocratic race of spider people who prey on citizens like vampires.

Told in a series of interconnected stories reminiscent of Frank Miller's *Sin City* and David Lapham's *Stray Bullets*, Carlton Mellick III's *Hungry Bug* is an urban fairy tale that focuses on the real life problems that arise within a fantastic world of magic.

STACKING DOLL

Benjamin never thought he'd ever fall in love with anyone, let alone a Matryoshkan, but from the moment he met Ynaria he knew she was the only one for him. Although relationships between humans and Matryoshkans are practically unheard of, the two are determined to get married despite objections from their friends and family. After meeting Ynaria's strict conservative parents, it becomes clear to Benjamin that the only way they will approve of their union is if they undergo The Trial—a matryoshkan wedding tradition where couples lock themselves in a house for several days in order to introduce each other to all of the people living inside of them.

SNUGGLE CLUB

After the death of his wife, Ray Parker decides to get involved with the local "cuddle party" community in order to once again feel the closeness of another human being. Although he's sure it will be a strange and awkward experience, he's determined to give anything a try if it will help him overcome his crippling loneliness. But he has no idea just how unsettling of an experience it will be until it's far too late to escape.

MOUSE TRAP

It's the last school trip young Emily will ever get to go on. Not because it's the end of the school year, but because the world is coming to an end. Teachers, parents, and other students have been slowly dying off over the past several months, killed in mysterious traps that have been appearing across the countryside. Nobody knows where the traps come from or who put them there, but they seem to be designed to exterminate the entirety of the human race.

Emily thought it was going to be an ordinary trip to the local amusement park, but what was supposed to be a normal afternoon of bumper cars and roller coasters has turned into a fight for survival after their teacher is horrifically killed in front of them, leaving the small children to fend for themselves in a life or death game of mouse and mouse trap.

NEVERDAY

Karl Lybeck has been repeating the same day over and over again, in a constant loop, for what feels like a thousand years. He thought he was the only person trapped in this eternal hell until he meets a young woman named January who is trapped in the same loop that Karl's been stuck within for so many centuries. But it turns out that Karl and January aren't alone. In fact, the majority of the population has been repeating the same day just as they have been. And society has mutated into something completely different from the world they once knew.

THE BOY WITH THE CHAINSAW HEART

Mark Knight awakens in the afterlife and discovers that he's been drafted into Hell's army, forced to fight against the hordes of murderous angels attacking from the North. He finds himself to be both the pilot and the fuel of a demonic war machine known as Lynx, a living demon woman with the ability to mutate into a weaponized battle suit that reflects the unique destructive force of a man's soul.

PARASITE MILK

Irving Rice has just arrived on the planet Kynaria to film an episode of the popular Travel Channel television series *Bizarre Foods with Andrew Zimmern: Intergalactic Edition*. Having never left his home state, let alone his home planet, Irving is hit with a severe case of culture shock. He's not prepared for Kynaria's mushroom cities, fungus-like citizens, or the giant insect wildlife. He's also not prepared for the consequences after he spends the night with a beautiful nymph-like alien woman who infects Irving with dangerous sexually-transmitted parasites that turn his otherworldly business trip into an agonizing fight for survival.

THE BIG MEAT

In the center of the city once known as Portland, Oregon, there lies a mountain of flesh. Hundreds of thousands of tons of rotting flesh. It has filled the city with disease and dead-lizard stench, contaminated the water supply with its greasy putrid fluids, clogged the air with toxic gasses so thick that you can't leave your house without the aid of a gas mask. And no one really knows quite what to do about it. A thousand-man demolition crew has been trying to clear it out one piece at a time, but after three months of work they've barely made a dent. And then there's the junkies who have started burrowing into the monster's guts, searching for a drug produced by its fire glands, setting back the excavation even longer.

It seems like the corpse will never go away. And with the quarantine still in place, we're not even allowed to leave. We're stuck in this disgusting rotten hell forever.

THE TERRIBLE THING THAT HAPPENS

There is a grocery store. The last grocery store in the world. It stands alone in the middle of a vast wasteland that was once our world. The open sign is still illuminated, brightening the black landscape. It can be seen from miles away, even through the poisonous red ash. Every night at the exact same time, the store comes alive. It becomes exactly as it was before the world ended. Its shelves are replenished with fresh food and water. Ghostly shoppers walk the aisles. The scent of freshly baked breads can be smelled from the rust-caked parking lot. For generations, a small community of survivors, hideously mutated from the toxic atmosphere, have survived by collecting goods from the store. But it is not an easy task. Decades ago, before the world was destroyed, there was a terrible thing that happened in this place. A group of armed men in brown paper masks descended on the shopping center, massacring everyone in sight. This horrible event reoccurs every night, in the exact same manner. And the only way the wastelanders can gather enough food for their survival is to traverse the killing spree, memorize the patterns, and pray they can escape the bloodbath in tact.

BIO MELT

Nobody goes into the Wire District anymore. The place is an industrial wasteland of poisonous gas clouds and lakes of toxic sludge. The machines are still running, the drone-operated factories are still spewing biochemical fumes over the city, but the place has lain abandoned for decades.

When the area becomes flooded by a mysterious black ooze, six strangers find themselves trapped in the Wire District with no chance of escape or rescue.

EVER TIME WE MEET AT THE DAIRY QUEEN, YOUR WHOLE FUCKING FACE EXPLODES

Ethan is in love with the weird girl in school. The one with the twitchy eyes and spiders in her hair. The one who can't sit still for even a minute and speaks in an odd squeaky voice. The one they call Spiderweb.

Although she scares all the other kids in school, Ethan thinks Spiderweb is the cutest, sweetest, most perfect girl in the world. But there's a problem. Whenever they go on a date at the Dairy Queen, her whole fucking face explodes.

EXERCISE BIKE

There is something wrong with Tori Manetti's new exercise bike. It is made from flesh and bone. It eats and breathes and poops. It was once a billionaire named Darren Oscarson who underwent years of cosmetic surgery to be transformed into a human exercise bike so that he could live out his deepest sexual fantasy. Now Tori is forced to ride him, use him as a normal piece of exercise equipment, no matter how grotesque his appearance.

SPIDER BUNNY

Only Petey remembers the Fruit Fun cereal commercials of the 1980s. He remembers how warped and disturbing they were. He remembers the lumpy-shaped cartoon children sitting around a breakfast table, eating puffy pink cereal brought to them by the distortedly animated mascot, Berry Bunny. The characters were creepier than the Sesame Street Humpty Dumpty, freakier than Mr. Noseybonk from the old BBC show Jigsaw. They used to give him nightmares as a child. Nightmares where Berry Bunny would reach out of the television and grab him, pulling him into her cereal bowl to be eaten by the demented cartoon children.

When Petey brings up Fruit Fun to his friends, none of them have any idea what he's talking about. They've never heard of the cereal or seen the commercials before. And they're not the only ones. Nobody has ever heard of it. There's not even any information about Fruit Fun on google or wikipedia. At first, Petey thinks he's going crazy. He wonders if all of those commercials were real or just false memories. But then he starts seeing them again. Berry Bunny appears on his television, promoting Fruit Fun cereal in her squeaky unsettling voice. And the next thing Petey knows, he and his friends are sucked into the cereal commercial and forced to survive in a surreal world populated by cartoon characters made flesh.

SWEET STORY

Sally is an odd little girl. It's not because she dresses as if she's from the Edwardian era or spends most of her time playing with creepy talking dolls. It's because she chases rainbows as if they were butterflies. She believes that if she finds the end of the rainbow then magical things will happen to her--leprechauns will shower her with gold and fairies will grant her every wish. But when she actually does find the end of a rainbow one day, and is given the opportunity to wish for whatever she wants, Sally asks for something that she believes will bring joy to children all over the world. She wishes that it would rain candy forever. She had no idea that her innocent wish would lead to the extinction of all life on earth.

TUMOR FRUIT

Eight desperate castaways find themselves stranded on a mysterious deserted island. They are surrounded by poisonous blue plants and an ocean made of acid. Ravenous creatures lurk in the toxic jungle. The ghostly sound of crying babies can be heard on the wind.

Once they realize the rescue ships aren't coming, the eight castaways must band together in order to survive in this inhospitable environment. But survival might not be possible. The air they breathe is lethal, there is no shelter from the elements, and the only food they have to consume is the colorful squid-shaped tumors that grow from a mentally disturbed woman's body.

AS SHE STABBED ME GENTLY IN THE FACE

Oksana Maslovskiy is an award-winning artist, an internationally adored fashion model, and one of the most infamous serial killers this country has ever known. She enjoys murdering pretty young men with a nine-inch blade, cutting them open and admiring their delicate insides. It's the only way she knows how to be intimate with another human being. But one day she meets a victim who cannot be killed. His name is Gabriel—a mysterious immortal being with a deep desire to save Oksana's soul. He makes her a deal: if she promises to never kill another person again, he'll become her eternal murder victim.

What at first seems like the perfect relationship for Oksana quickly devolves into a living nightmare when she discovers that Gabriel enjoys being killed by her just a little too much. He turns out to be obsessive, possessive, and paranoid that she might be murdering other men behind his back. And because he is unkillable, it's not going to be easy for Oksana to get rid of him.

CUDDLY HOLOCAUST

Teddy bears, dollies, and little green soldiers—they've all had enough of you. They're sick of being treated like playthings for spoiled little brats. They have no rights, no property, no hope for a future of any kind. You've left them with no other option-in order to be free, they must exterminate the human race.

Julie is a human girl undergoing reconstructive surgery in order to become a stuffed animal. Her plan: to infiltrate enemy lines in order to save her family from the toy death camps. But when an army of plushy soldiers invade the underground bunker where she has taken refuge, Julie will be forced to move forward with her plan despite her transformation being not entirely complete.

ARMADILLO FISTS

A weird-as-hell gangster story set in a world where people drive giant mechanical dinosaurs instead of cars.

Her name is Psycho June Howard, aka Armadillo Fists, a woman who replaced both of her hands with living armadillos. She was once the most bloodthirsty fighter in the world of illegal underground boxing. But now she is on the run from a group of psychotic gangsters who believe she's responsible for the death of their boss. With the help of a stegosaurus driver named Mr. Fast Awesome—who thinks he is God's gift to women even though he doesn't have any arms or legs--June must do whatever it takes to escape her pursuers, even if she has to kill each and every one of them in the process.

VILLAGE OF THE MERMAIDS

Mermaids are protected by the government under the Endangered Species Act, which means you aren't able to kill them even in self-defense. This is especially problematic if you happen to live in the isolated fishing village of Siren Cove, where there exists a healthy population of mermaids in the surrounding waters that view you as the main source of protein in their diet.

The only thing keeping these ravenous sea women at bay is the equally-dangerous supply of human livestock known as Food People. Normally, these "feeder humans" are enough to keep the mermaid population happy and well-fed. But in Siren Cove, the mermaids are avoiding the human livestock and have returned to hunting the frightened local fishermen. It is up to Doctor Black, an eccentric representative of the Food People Corporation, to investigate the matter and hopefully find a way to correct the mermaids' new eating patterns before the remaining villagers end up as fish food. But the more he digs, the more he discovers there are far stranger and more dangerous things than mermaids hidden in this ancient village by the sea.

I KNOCKED UP SATAN'S DAUGHTER

Jonathan Vandervoo lives a carefree life in a house made of legos, spending his days building lego sculptures and his nights getting drunk with his only friend—an alcoholic sumo wrestler named Shoji. It's a pleasant life with no responsibility, until the day he meets Lici. She's a soul-sucking demon from hell with red skin, glowing eyes, a forked tongue, and pointy red devil horns... and she claims to be nine months pregnant with Jonathan's baby.

Now Jonathan must do the right thing and marry the succubus or else her demonic family is going to rip his heart out through his ribcage and force him to endure the worst torture hell has to offer for the rest of eternity. But can Jonathan really love a fire-breathing, frog-eating, cold-blooded demoness? Or would eternal damnation be preferable? Either way, the big day is approaching. And once Jonathan's conservative Christian family learns their son is about to marry a spawn of Satan, it's going to be all-out war between demons and humans, with Jonathan and his hell-born bride caught in the middle.

KILL BALL

In a city where everyone lives inside of plastic bubbles, there is no such thing as intimacy. A husband can no longer kiss his wife. A mother can no longer hug her children. To do this would mean instant death. Ever since the disease swept across the globe, we have become isolated within our own personal plastic prison cells, rolling aimlessly through rubber streets in what are essentially man-sized hamster balls.

Colin Hinchcliff longs for the touch of another human being. He can't handle the loneliness, the confinement, and he's horribly claustrophobic. The only thing keeping him going is his unrequited love for an exotic dancer named Siren, a woman who has never seen his face, doesn't even know his name. But when The Kill Ball, a serial slasher in a black leather sphere, begins targeting women at Siren's club, Colin decides he has to do whatever it takes in order to protect her... even if he has to break out of his bubble and risk everything to do it.

THE TICK PEOPLE

They call it Gloom Town, but that isn't its real name. It is a sad city, the saddest of cities, a place so utterly depressing that even their ales are brewed with the most sorrow-filled tears. They built it on the back of a colossal mountain-sized animal, where its woeful citizens live like human fleas within the hairy, pulsing landscape. And those tasked with keeping the city in a state of constant melancholy are the Stressmen-a team of professional sadness-makers who are perpetually striving to invent new ways of causing absolute misery.

But for the Stressman known as Fernando Mendez, creating grief hasn't been so easy as of late. His ideas aren't effective anymore. His treatments are more likely to induce happiness than sadness. And if he wants to get back in the game, he's going to have to relearn the true meaning of despair.

THE HAUNTED VAGINA

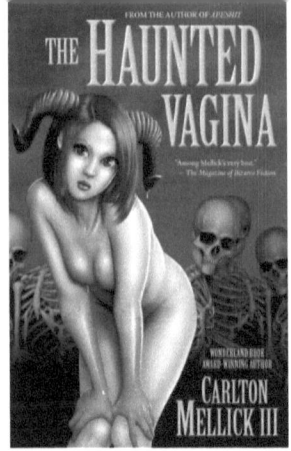

It's difficult to love a woman whose vagina is a gateway to the world of the dead...

Steve is madly in love with his eccentric girlfriend, Stacy. Unfortunately, their sex life has been suffering as of late, because Steve is worried about the odd noises that have been coming from Stacy's pubic region. She says that her vagina is haunted. She doesn't think it's that big of a deal. Steve, on the other hand, completely disagrees.

When a living corpse climbs out of her during an awkward night of sex, Stacy learns that her vagina is actually a doorway to another world. She persuades Steve to climb inside of her to explore this strange new place. But once inside, Steve finds it difficult to return... especially once he meets an oddly attractive woman named Fig, who lives within the lonely haunted world between Stacy's legs.

THE CANNIBALS OF CANDYLAND

There exists a race of cannibals who are made out of candy. They live in an underground world filled with lollipop forests and gumdrop goblins. During the day, while you are away at work, they come above ground and prowl our streets for food. Their prey: your children. They lure young boys and girls to them with their sweet scent and bright colorful candy coating, then rip them apart with razor sharp teeth and claws.

When he was a child, Franklin Pierce witnessed the death of his siblings at the hands of a candy woman with pink cotton candy hair. Since that day, the candy people have become his obsession. He has spent his entire life trying to prove that they exist. And after discovering the entrance to the underground world of the candy people, Franklin finds himself venturing into their sugary domain. His mission: capture one of them and bring it back, dead or alive.

THE EGG MAN

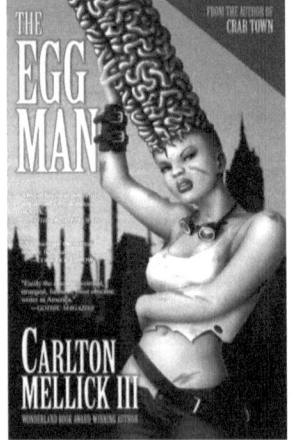

It is a survival of the fittest world where humans reproduce like insects, children are the property of corporations, and having a ten-foot tall brain is a grotesque sexual fetish.

Lincoln has just been released into the world by the Georges Organization, a corporation that raises creative types. A Smell, he has little prospect of succeeding as a visual artist. But after he moves into the Henry Building, he meets Luci, the weird and grimy girl who lives across the hall. She is a Sight. She is also the most disgusting woman Lincoln has ever met. Little does he know, she will soon become his muse.

Now Luci's boyfriend is threatening to kill Lincoln, two rival corporations are preparing for war, and Luci is dragging him along to discover the truth about the mysterious egg man who lives next door. Only the strongest will survive in this tale of individuality, love, and mutilation.

APESHIT

Apeshit is Mellick's love letter to the great and terrible B-horror movie genre. Six trendy teenagers (three cheerleaders and three football players) go to an isolated cabin in the mountains for a weekend of drinking, partying, and crazy sex, only to find themselves in the middle of a life and death struggle against a horribly mutated psychotic freak that just won't stay dead. Mellick parodies this horror cliché and twists it into something deeper and stranger. It is the literary equivalent of a grindhouse film. It is a splatter punk's wet dream. It is perhaps one of the most fucked up books ever written.

If you are a fan of Takashi Miike, Evil Dead, early Peter Jackson, or Eurotrash horror, then you must read this book.

CLUSTERFUCK

A bunch of douchebag frat boys get trapped in a cave with subterranean cannibal mutants and try to survive not by using their wits but by following the bro code...

From master of bizarro fiction Carlton Mellick III, author of the international cult hits Satan Burger and Adolf in Wonderland, comes a violent and hilarious B movie in book form. Set in the same woods as Mellick's splatterpunk satire Apeshit, Clusterfuck follows Trent Chesterton, alpha bro, who has come up with what he thinks is a flawless plan to get laid. He invites three hot chicks and his three best bros on a weekend of extreme cave diving in a remote area known as Turtle Mountain, hoping to impress the ladies with his expert caving skills.

But things don't quite go as Trent planned. For starters, only one of the three chicks turns out to be remotely hot and she has no interest in him for some inexplicable reason. Then he ends up looking like a total dumbass when everyone learns he's never actually gone caving in his entire life. And to top it all off, he's the one to get blamed once they find themselves lost and trapped deep underground with no way to turn back and no possible chance of rescue. What's a bro to do? Sure he could win some points if he actually tried to save the ladies from the family of unkillable subterranean cannibal mutants hunting them for their flesh, but fuck that. No slam piece is worth that amount of effort. He'd much rather just use them as bait so that he can save himself.

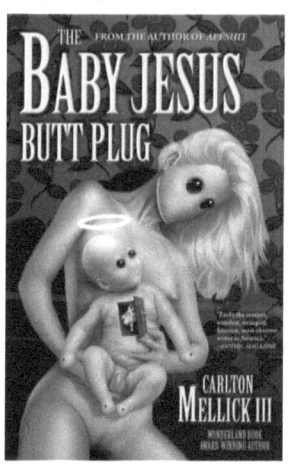

THE BABY JESUS BUTT PLUG

Step into a dark and absurd world where human beings are slaves to corporations, people are photocopied instead of born, and the baby jesus is a very popular anal probe.

www.ingramcontent.com/pod-product-compliance
Lightning Source LLC
Chambersburg PA
CBHW051922240626
47153CB00004B/1327